DOCTOR BRODIE'S REPORT

DOCTOR BRODIE'S REPORT

JORGE LUIS BORGES

Translated by
Norman Thomas
di Giovanni
in collaboration
with the author

A Dutton Paperback
E. P. Dutton   *New York*

The translations in this volume made their first appearances
in the following periodicals:
The Atlantic Monthly: "Doctor Brodie's Report"
Buenos Aires Herald: "The Intruder"
Harper's Magazine: "The Unworthy Friend"
Mundus Artium: "The Duel"
New American Review: "Guayaquil"
The New Yorker: "The Meeting," "The End of the Duel," "Juan
Muraña," "The Elder Lady," "The Gospel According to Mark"
"Rosendo's Tale" was first published in *The Aleph and Other Stories
1933-1969,* E. P. Dutton & Co., New York, 1970.
The Preface, under the title "Borges on Borges," first appeared in *The
New York Review of Books.*

This paperback edition first published in 1978 by E. P. Dutton, a Division of Sequoia-
Elsevier Publishing Company, Inc., New York

Published simultaneously in Canada
by Clarke, Irwin & Company Limited, Toronto and Vancouver
Library of Congress Catalog Card Number: 72-158581
ISBN: 0-525-47541-9

10 9 8 7 6 5 4 3 2 1

Contents

Foreword 7

Preface to the First Edition 9

The Gospel According to Mark 15

The Unworthy Friend 25

The Duel 35

The End of the Duel 45

Rosendo's Tale 53

The Intruder 63

The Meeting 71

Juan Muraña 81

The Elder Lady 89

Guayaquil 99

Doctor Brodie's Report 111

Afterword 123

Bibliographical Note 127

Foreword

The principle we have followed in translating this book is, of course, the same used in our previous Dutton volume, *The Aleph and Other Stories 1933–1969*. There our guiding aim had been to make the text read as though it had been written in English; in so doing, we quite soon discovered that the English and Spanish languages are not, as is often taken for granted, a set of interchangeable synonyms but are two possible ways of viewing and ordering reality. We have also continued in the present volume to supply the American reader with historical and geographical details not necessarily known to him.

One difference between this volume and the last lies in the fact that the writing and the translation were, except in one case, more or less simultaneous. In this way our work was easier for us, since, as we were always under the spell of the originals, we stood in no need of trying to recapture past moods. This seems to us to be the best possible condition under which to practice the craft of translation.

The Afterword, written directly in English, was prepared especially for this volume.

J. L. B.
N. T. di G.

Buenos Aires, December 29, 1970

Preface to the First Edition

Kipling's last stories were no less tormented and mazelike than the stories of Kafka or Henry James, which they doubtless surpass; but in 1885, in Lahore, the young Kipling began a series of brief tales, written in a straightforward manner, that he was to collect in 1890. Several of them—"In the House of Suddhoo," "Beyond the Pale," "The Gate of the Hundred Sorrows"—are laconic masterpieces. It occurred to me that what was conceived and carried out by a young man of genius might modestly be attempted by a man on the borders of old age who knows his craft. Out of that idea came the present volume, which I leave to the reader to judge.

I have done my best—I don't know with what success—to write straightforward stories. I do not dare state that they are simple; there isn't anywhere on earth a single page or single word that is, since each thing implies the universe, whose most obvious trait is complexity. I want to make it quite clear that I am not, nor have I ever been, what used to be called a preacher of parables or a fabulist and is now known as a committed writer. I do not aspire to be Aesop. My stories, like those of the Thousand and One Nights, try to be entertaining or moving but not persuasive. Such an intention does not mean that I have shut myself up, according to Solomon's image, in an ivory tower. My political convictions are quite well known; I am a member of the Conservative Party— this in itself is a form of skepticism—and no one has ever branded me a Communist, a nationalist, an anti-Semite, a follower of Billy the Kid or of the dictator Rosas. I believe that some day we will deserve not to have governments. I have never kept my opinions hidden, not even in trying times, but neither have I ever allowed them to find their way into my literary work, except once when I was buoyed up in exultation over the Six-Day War. The art of writing is mysterious; the opinions we hold are ephemeral, and I prefer the Platonic idea of the Muse to that of Poe, who reasoned, or feigned to reason, that the writing of a poem is an act of the intelligence. It never fails to amaze me that the classics hold a romantic theory of poetry, and a romantic poet a classical theory.

Apart from the text that gives this book its title and that obviously derives from Lemuel Gulliver's last voyage, my stories are—to use the term in vogue today—realistic. They follow, I believe, all the conventions of that school, which is as conventional as any other and of which we shall soon grow tired if we have not already done so. They are rich in the required invention of circumstances. Splendid examples of this device are to be found in the tenth-century Old English ballad of Maldon and in the later Icelandic sagas. Two stories—I will not give their names—hold the same fantastic key. The curious reader will notice certain close affinities between them. The same few plots, I am sorry to say, have pursued me down through the years; I am decidedly monotonous.

I owe to a dream of Hugo Rodríguez Moroni the general

outline of the story—perhaps the best of this collection—called "The Gospel According to Mark." I fear having spoiled it with the changes that my fancy or my reason judged fitting. But after all, writing is nothing more than a guided dream.

I have given up the surprises inherent in a baroque style as well as the surprises that lead to an unforeseen ending. I have, in short, preferred to satisfy an expectation rather than to provide a startling shock. For many years, I thought it might be given me to achieve a good page by means of variations and novelties; now, having passed seventy, I believe I have found my own voice. Slight rewording neither spoils nor improves what I dictate, except in cases of lightening a clumsy sentence or toning down an exaggeration. Each language is a tradition, each word a shared symbol, and what an innovator can change amounts to a trifle; we need only remember the splendid but often unreadable work of a Mallarmé or a Joyce. It is likely that this all-too-reasonable reasoning is only the fruit of weariness. My now advanced age has taught me to resign myself to being Borges.

I am impartially indifferent to both the dictionary of the Spanish Royal Academy—*dont chaque édition fait regretter la précédente*, according to the sad observation of Paul Groussac—and those weighty Argentine dictionaries of local usage. All, I find—those of this and those of the other side of the ocean—have a tendency to emphasize differences and to fragment the Spanish language. In connection with this, I recall that when it was held against the novelist Roberto Arlt that he had no knowledge of Buenos Aires slang, he replied, "I grew up in Villa Luro, among poor people and hoodlums, and I really had no time to learn that sort of thing." Our local slang, in fact, is a literary joke concocted by writers of popular plays and tango lyrics, and the people who are supposed to use it hardly know what it means, except when they have been indoctrinated by phonograph records.

I have set my stories some distance off in time and in space. The imagination, in this way, can operate with greater freedom. Who, in 1970, is able to remember with accuracy what at the end of the last century the outskirts of Buenos Aires around Palermo and Lomas were like? Unbelievable as it may seem, there are those who go to the length of playing policeman and looking for a writer's petty slips. They remark, for example, that Martín Fierro would have spoken of a "bag" and not a "sack" of bones, and they find fault, perhaps unjustly, with the roan piebald coat of a certain horse famous in our literature.

God spare thee, reader, long prefaces. The words are Quevedo's, who, careful not to fall into an anachronism which in the long run would have been detected, never read those of Bernard Shaw.

J. L. B.

Buenos Aires, April 19, 1970

The Gospel According to Mark

The Gospel According to Mark

These events took place at La Colorada ranch, in the south-
ern part of the township of Junín, during the last days of
March, 1928. The protagonist was a medical student named
Baltasar Espinosa. We may describe him, for now, as one of
the common run of young men from Buenos Aires, with
nothing more noteworthy about him than an almost unlim-
ited kindness and a capacity for public speaking that had
earned him several prizes at the English school in Ramos
Mejía. He did not like arguing, and preferred having his lis-
tener rather than himself in the right. Although he was fasci-
nated by the probabilities of chance in any game he played,
he was a bad player because it gave him no pleasure to win.
His wide intelligence was undirected; at the age of thirty-
three, he still lacked credit for graduation, by one course—
the course to which he was most drawn. His father, who
was a freethinker (like all the gentlemen of his day), had in-
troduced him to the lessons of Herbert Spencer, but his
mother, before leaving on a trip to Montevideo, once asked
him to say the Lord's Prayer and make the sign of the cross

every night. Through the years, he had never gone back on that promise.

Espinosa was not lacking in spirit; one day, with more indifference than anger, he had exchanged two of three punches with a group of fellow-students who were trying to force him to take part in a university demonstration. Owing to an acquiescent nature, he was full of opinions, or habits of mind, that were questionable: Argentina mattered less to him than a fear that in other parts of the world people might think of us as Indians; he worshiped France but despised the French; he thought little of Americans but approved the fact that there were tall buildings, like theirs, in Buenos Aires; he believed the gauchos of the plains to be better riders than those of hill or mountain country. When his cousin Daniel invited him to spend the summer months out at La Colorada, he said yes at once—not because he was really fond of the country, but more out of his natural complacency and also because it was easier to say yes than to dream up reasons for saying no.

The ranch's main house was big and slightly run-down; the quarters of the foreman, whose name was Gutre, were close by. The Gutres were three: the father, an unusually uncouth son, and a daughter of uncertain paternity. They were tall, strong, and bony, and had hair that was on the reddish side and faces that showed traces of Indian blood. They were barely articulate. The foreman's wife had died years before.

There in the country, Espinosa began learning things he never knew, or even suspected—for example, that you do not gallop a horse when approaching settlements, and that you never go out riding except for some special purpose. In time, he was to come to tell the birds apart by their calls.

After a few days, Daniel had to leave for Buenos Aires to close a deal on some cattle. At most, this bit of business might take him a week. Espinosa, who was already some-what weary of hearing about his cousin's incessant luck with women and his tireless interest in the minute details of men's fashion, preferred staying on at the ranch with his textbooks. But the heat was unbearable, and even the night brought no relief. One morning at daybreak, thunder woke him. Out-side, the wind was rocking the Australian pines. Listening to the first heavy drops of rain, Espinosa thanked God. All at once, cold air rolled in. That afternoon, the Salado over-flowed its banks.

The next day, looking out over the flooded fields from the gallery of the main house, Baltasar Espinosa thought that the stock metaphor comparing the pampa to the sea was not alto-gether false—at least, not that morning—though W. H. Hudson had remarked that the sea seems wider because we view it from a ship's deck and not from a horse or from eye level.

The rain did not let up. The Gutres, helped or hindered by Espinosa, the town dweller, rescued a good part of the live-stock, but many animals were drowned. There were four roads leading to La Colorada; all of them were under water. On the third day, when a leak threatened the foreman's house, Espinosa gave the Gutres a room near the tool shed, at the back of the main house. This drew them all closer; they ate together in the big dining room. Conversation turned out to be difficult. The Gutres, who knew so much about coun-try things, were hard put to it to explain them. One night, Espinosa asked them if people still remembered the Indian raids from back when the frontier command was located there in Junín. They told him yes, but they would have given the same answer to a question about the beheading of Charles I. Espinosa recalled his father's saying that almost every case of longevity that was cited in the country was really a case of bad memory or of a dim notion of dates. Gauchos are apt to be ignorant of the year of their birth or of the name of the man who begot them.

In the whole house, there was apparently no other reading matter than a set of the *Farm Journal*, a handbook of veterinary medicine, a deluxe edition of the Uruguayan epic *Tabaré*, a *History of Shorthorn Cattle in Argentina*, a number of erotic or detective stories, and a recent novel called *Don Segundo Sombra*. Espinosa, trying in some way to bridge the inevitable after-dinner gap, read a couple of chapters of this novel to the Gutres, none of whom could read or write. Unfortunately, the foreman had been a cattle drover, and the doings of the hero, another cattle drover, failed to whet his interest. He said that the work was light, that drovers always traveled with a packhorse that carried everything they needed, and that, had he not been a drover, he would never have seen such far-flung places as the Laguna de Gómez, the town of Bragado, and the spread of the Núñez family in Chacabuco. There was a guitar in the kitchen; the ranch hands, before the time of the events I am describing, used to sit around in a circle. Someone would tune the instrument without ever getting around to playing it. This was known as a guitarfest.

Espinosa, who had grown a beard, began dallying in front of the mirror to study his new face, and he smiled to think how, back in Buenos Aires, he would bore his friends by telling them the story of the Salado flood. Strangely enough, he missed places he never frequented and never would: a corner of Cabrera Street on which there was a mailbox; one of the cement lions of a gateway on Jujuy Street, a few blocks from the Plaza del Once; an old barroom with a tiled floor, whose exact whereabouts he was unsure of. As for his brothers and his father, they would already have learned from Daniel that he was isolated—etymologically, the word was perfect—by the floodwaters.

Exploring the house, still hemmed in by the watery waste, Espinosa came across an English Bible. Among the blank pages at the end, the Guthries—such was their original name—had left a handwritten record of their lineage. They were natives of Inverness; had reached the New World, no doubt as common laborers, in the early part of the nineteenth century; and had intermarried with Indians. The chronicle broke off sometime during the eighteen-seventies, when they no longer knew how to write. After a few generations, they had forgotten English; their Spanish, at the time Espinosa knew them, gave them trouble. They lacked any religious faith, but there survived in their blood, like faint tracks, the rigid fanaticism of the Calvinist and the superstitions of the pampa Indian. Espinosa later told them of his find, but they barely took notice.

Leafing through the volume, his fingers opened it at the beginning of the Gospel according to St. Mark. As an exercise in translation, and maybe to find out whether the Gutres understood any of it, Espinosa decided to begin reading them that text after their evening meal. It surprised him that they listened attentively, absorbed. Maybe the gold letters on the cover lent the book authority. It's still there in their blood, Espinosa thought. It also occurred to him that the generations of men, throughout recorded time, have always told and retold two stories—that of a lost ship which searches the Mediterranean seas for a dearly loved island, and that of a god who is crucified on Golgotha. Remembering his lessons in elocution from his schooldays in Ramos Mejía, Espinosa got to his feet when he came to the parables.

The Gutres took to bolting their barbecued meat and their sardines so as not to delay the Gospel. A pet lamb that the girl adorned with a small blue ribbon had injured itself on a strand of barbed wire. To stop the bleeding, the three had wanted to apply a cobweb to the wound, but Espinosa treated the animal with some pills. The gratitude that this treatment awakened in them took him aback. (Not trusting the Gutres at first, he'd hidden away in one of his books the two hundred and forty pesos he had brought with him.) Now, the owner of the place away, Espinosa took over and gave timid orders, which were immediately obeyed. The Gutres, as if lost without him, liked following him from room to room and along the gallery that ran around the house. While he read to them, he noticed that they were secretly stealing the crumbs he had dropped on the table. One evening, he caught them unawares, talking about him respectfully, in very few words.

Having finished the Gospel according to St. Mark, he wanted to read another of the three Gospels that remained, but the father asked him to repeat the one he had just read, so that they could understand it better. Espinosa felt that they were like children, to whom repetition is more pleasing than variations or novelty. That night—this is not to be wondered at—he dreamed of the Flood; the hammer blows of the building of the Ark woke him up, and he thought that perhaps they were thunder. In fact, the rain, which had let up, started again. The cold was bitter. The Gutres had told him that the storm had damaged the roof of the tool shed, and that they would show it to him when the beams were fixed. No longer a stranger now, he was treated by them with special attention, almost to the point of spoiling him. None of them liked coffee, but for him there was always a small cup into which they heaped sugar.

The new storm had broken out on a Tuesday. Thursday night, Espinosa was awakened by a soft knock at his door, which—just in case—he always kept locked. He got out of bed and opened it; there was the girl. In the dark he could hardly make her out, but by her footsteps he could tell she was barefoot, and moments later, in bed, that she must have come all the way from the other end of the house naked. She did not embrace him or speak a single word; she lay beside him, trembling. It was the first time she had known a man. When she left, she did not kiss him; Espinosa realized that he didn't even know her name. For some reason that he did not want to pry into, he made up his mind that upon returning to Buenos Aires he would tell no one about what had taken place.

The next day began like the previous ones, except that the father spoke to Espinosa and asked him if Christ had let Himself be killed so as to save all other men on earth. Espinosa, who was a freethinker but who felt committed to what he had read to the Gutres, answered, "Yes, to save everyone from Hell."

Gutre then asked, "What's Hell?"

"A place under the ground where souls burn and burn."

"And the Roman soldiers who hammered in the nails— were they saved, too?"

"Yes," said Espinosa, whose theology was rather dim.

All along, he was afraid that the foreman might ask him about what had gone on the night before with his daughter. After lunch, they asked him to read the last chapters over again.

Espinosa slept a long nap that afternoon. It was a light sleep, disturbed by persistent hammering and by vague premonitions. Toward evening, he got up and went out onto the gallery. He said, as if thinking aloud, "The waters have dropped. It won't be long now."

"It won't be long now," Gutre repeated, like an echo.

The three had been following him. Bowing their knees to the stone pavement, they asked his blessing. Then they mocked at him, spat on him, and shoved him toward the back part of the house. The girl wept. Espinosa understood what awaited him on the other side of the door. When they opened it, he saw a patch of sky. A bird sang out. A gold-finch, he thought. The shed was without a roof; they had pulled down the beams to make the cross.

The Unworthy Friend

The Unworthy Friend

Our image of the city is always slightly out of date. Cafés have degenerated into barrooms; old arched entranceways with their grilled inner gates, once giving us a glimpse of patios and of overhanging grapevines, are now dingy corridors that lead abruptly to an elevator. For years, in this way, I thought that in a certain block of Talcahuano Street I might still find the Buenos Aires Bookstore. But one morning I discovered its place had been taken by an antique shop, and I was told that don Santiago Fischbein, its owner, had died. Fischbein had been a heavyset, rather overweight man, whose features I now remember less than our long talks. In a quiet but firm way he had always been against Zionism, which he held would turn the Jew into a man like anyone else—tied down to a single tradition and a single homeland, and no longer enriched by strife and complexities. He'd been at work, he once told me, putting together a comprehensive anthology of the writings of Baruch Spinoza, freed of all that Euclidean apparatus, which, while lending to its strange system an illusory rigor, bogs the reader down. He would not sell me, but let me look at, a rare copy of Rosenroth's *Kabbala Denudata*. At home I still have a few books on the Kabbalah by Ginsburg and by Waite which bear the seal of Fischbein's shop.

One afternoon, when the two of us were alone, he confided a story to me about his early life, and I feel I can now set it down. As may be expected, I will alter one or two details. Here is what Fischbein said.

———

I'm going to tell you something I've never told anyone before. Ana—my wife—doesn't know a word about this, nor do any of my closest friends. These things took place so many years ago now that I sometimes feel they might have happened to another person. Maybe you can make some use of this as a story—which, of course, you'll dress up with daggers. I wonder if I've already told you I was born in the Province of Entre Ríos. I can't say we were Jewish gauchos —there never were any Jewish gauchos. We were shopkeepers and farmers. Anyway, I was born in Urdinarrain, a town I can hardly remember anymore. I was very young when my parents moved to Buenos Aires to open up a shop. A few blocks away from where we lived was the Maldonado, and beyond that ditch were open lots.

Carlyle says that men need heroes to worship. Argentine schoolbooks tried getting me to worship San Martín, but in him I found little more than a soldier who'd fought his battles in other countries and who's now only a bronze statue and the name of a square. Chance, however—unfortunately enough for the two of us—provided me with another kind of hero. This is probably the first time you've ever heard of him. His name was Francisco Ferrari.

Our neighborhood may not have been as tough as the Stockyards or the waterfront, but it had its share of hoodlums who hung out in the old saloons. Ferrari's particular hangout was a place at the corner of Triunvirato and Thames. It was there the thing happened that brought me under his spell. I'd been sent around to the saloon to buy a small package of maté, when in walked a stranger with long hair and a moustache, and ordered a shot of gin. Ferrari said to him, mildly, "By the way, didn't we see each other night before last dancing at Juliana's? Where are you from?"

"From San Cristóbal," the other man said.

"My advice," Ferrari said, still gently, "is that you might find it healthier to keep away from here. This neighborhood's full of people on the lookout for trouble."

On the spot, the man from San Cristóbal turned tail—moustache and all. Maybe he was just as much a man as Ferrari was, but he knew others of the gang were around.

From that afternoon on, Francisco Ferrari was the hero my fifteen years were in search of. He was dark and stood straight and tall—good-looking in the style of the day. He always wore black. One day, a second episode brought us together. I was on the street with my mother and aunt, when we ran into a bunch of young toughs and one of them said loudly to the others:

"Old stuff. Let them by."

I didn't know what to do. At that moment, Ferrari stepped in. He had just left his house. He looked the ringleader straight in the eye and said, "If you're out for fun, why not try having some with me?"

He kept staring them up and down, one after the other, and there wasn't a word out of any of them. They knew all about him. Ferrari shrugged his shoulders, tipped his hat, and went on his way. But before starting off, he said to me, "If you have nothing else to do, drop in at the saloon later on."

I was tongue-tied. "There's a gentleman who demands respect for ladies," my Aunt Sarah pronounced.

Coming to my rescue, my mother said, "I'd say more a hoodlum who wants no competition."

I don't really know how to explain this now. I've worked my way up, I own this shop—which I love—and I know my books; I enjoy friendships like ours, I have my wife and children, I belong to the Socialist Party, I'm a good Argentine and a good Jew. People look up to me. As you can see, I'm almost bald; in those days I was just a poor redheaded Jew-boy, living in a down-and-out neighborhood. Like all young men, of course, I tried hard to be the same as everyone else. Still, I was sneered at. To shake off the Jacob, I called myself Santiago, but just the same there was the Fischbein. We all begin taking on the idea others have of us. Feeling people despised me, I despised myself as well. At that time, and above all in that neighborhood, you had to be tough. I knew I was a coward. Women scared the daylights out of me, I was deeply ashamed of my inexperience with them, and I had no friends my own age.

That night I didn't go around to the saloon. How I wish I never had! But the feeling grew on me that Ferrari's invitation was something of an order, so the next Saturday, after dinner, I finally walked into the place.

Ferrari sat at the head of one of the tables. I knew all the other men by sight. There were six or seven of them. Ferrari was the eldest, except for an old man who spoke little and wearily and whose name is the only one I have not forgotten—don Eliseo Amaro. The mark of a slash crossed his broad, flabby face. I found out afterward he'd spent some time in jail.

Ferrari sat me down at his left, making don Eliseo change places for me. I felt a bit uneasy, afraid Ferrari would mention what had happened on the street a few days before. But nothing of the kind took place. They talked of women, cards, elections, of a street singer who was about to show up but

never did, of neighborhood affairs. At first, they seemed un-
willing to accept me, then later—because it was what Ferrari wanted—they loosened up. In spite of their names,
which for the most part were Italian, every one of them
thought of himself (and thought of each other) as Argentine
and even gaucho. Some of them owned or drove teams or
were butchers at the slaughter yards, and having to deal with
animals made them a lot like farm hands. My suspicion is that
their one desire was to have played the outlaw Juan Moreira.
They ended up calling me the Sheeny, but they didn't mean
it in a bad way. It was from them that I learned to smoke and
do other things.

In a brothel on Junín Street, somebody asked me whether I
wasn't a friend of Francisco Ferrari's. I told him I wasn't,
feeling that to have answered yes would have been bragging.

One night the police came into the saloon and frisked us.
Two of the gang were taken into custody, but Ferrari was
left alone. A couple of weeks later the same thing happened
all over again; this second time they rounded up Ferrari, too.
Under his belt he was carrying a knife. What happened was
that he must have had a falling out with the political boss of
our ward.

As I look back on Ferrari today, I see him as an unlucky
young man who was filled with illusions and in the end was
betrayed; but at the time, to me he was a god.

Friendship is no less a mystery than love or any other as-
pect of this confusion we call life. There have been times
when I've felt the only thing without mystery is happiness,
because happiness is an end in itself. The plain fact is that, for
all his brass, Francisco Ferrari, the tough guy, wanted to be
friends with someone as pitiful as me. I was sure he'd made a
mistake, I was sure I was unworthy of his friendship, and I
did my best to keep clear of him. But he wouldn't let me. My
anxiety over this was made even worse by my mother's disap-

proval. She just couldn't get used to the company I kept and went around aping, and referred to them as trash and scum. The point of what I'm telling you is my relationship with Ferrari, not the sordid facts, which I no longer feel sorry about. As long as any trace of remorse remains, guilt remains.

One night, the old man, who had again taken up his usual place beside Ferrari, was whispering back and forth in Ferrari's ear. They were up to something. From the other end of the table, I thought I made out the name of Weidemann, a man who owned a textile mill out on the edge of the neighborhood. Soon after, without any explanation, I was told to take a stroll around Weidemann's factory and to have a good look at the gates. It was beginning to get dark when I crossed the Maldonado and cut through the freight yards. I remember the houses, which grew fewer and farther between, a clump of willows, and the empty lots. Weidemann's was new, but it was lonely and somehow looked like a ruin; in my memory, its red brick gets mixed up with the sunset. The mill was surrounded by a tall fence. In addition to the front entrance, there were two big doors out back opening into the south side of the building.

I have to admit it took me some time to figure out what you've probably guessed already. I brought back my report, which was confirmed by one of the others, who had a sister working in the place. Then the plan was laid out. For the gang not to have shown up at the saloon on a Saturday night would have attracted attention, so Ferrari set the robbery for the following Friday. I was the one they picked for lookout. Meanwhile, it was best that we shouldn't be seen together. When we were alone in the street—just Ferrari and myself—I asked him, "Are you sure you can trust me?"

"Yes," he answered. "I know you'll handle yourself like a man."

That night and the following nights I slept well. Then, on

Wednesday, I told my mother I was going downtown to see a new cowboy picture. I put on my best clothes and started out for Moreno Street. The trip on the streetcar was a long one. At police headquarters I was kept waiting, but finally one of the desk sergeants—a certain Eald or Alt—saw me. I told him I'd come about a confidential matter and he said I could speak without fear. I let him in on the gang's plan. What surprised me was that Ferrari's name meant nothing to him; but it was something else again when I mentioned don Eliseo.

"Ah," he said. "He used to be one of the old Montevideo gang."

He called in another man, who came from my part of town, and the two of them talked things over. The second officer asked me, with a certain scorn in his voice, "Have you come here with this information because you think of yourself as a good citizen?"

I knew he would never understand, but I answered, "Yes, sir. I'm a good Argentine."

They told me to go through with my job exactly as Ferrari had ordered, but not to whistle when I saw the police arrive. As I was leaving, one of them warned me:

"Better be careful. You know what happens to stoolies."

Policemen are just like kids when it comes to using slang. I answered him, "I wish they would lay their hands on me— maybe that's the best thing that could happen."

From early in the morning that Friday, I had the feeling of relief that the day had come, and at the same time I felt the guilt of not feeling guilty. The hours seemed to drag. All day I barely ate a mouthful. At ten that night we met a couple of blocks away from the factory. When one of the gang didn't show up, don Eliseo remarked that someone always turned yellow. I knew when it was over he'd be the one they'd blame.

It looked like it was about to pour. At first, I was scared someone else would be named to stand watch with me, but when it came time I was left alone near one of the back doors. After a while, the police, together with a superior officer, put in their appearance. They came on foot, having left their horses some distance off. Ferrari had forced one of the two doors and the police were able to slip in without a sound. Then four shots rang out, deafening me. I imagined that there on the inside, in all that dark, they were slaughtering each other. At that point the police led a few of the men out in handcuffs. Then two more policemen came out, dragging the bodies of Francisco Ferrari and don Eliseo Amaro. In the official report it was stated that they had resisted arrest and had been the first to open fire. I knew the whole thing was a lie because I'd never once seen any of the gang carrying guns. They'd just been shot down; the police had used the occasion to settle an old score. A few days later, I heard that Ferrari had tried to escape but had been stopped by a single bullet. As was to be expected, the newspapers made the hero of him he had never been except maybe in my eyes.

As for me, they rounded me up with the others and a short time later set me free.

The Duel

To Juan Osvaldo Viviano

The Duel

Henry James—whose world was first revealed to me by one of my two characters, Clara Figueroa—would perhaps have been interested in this story. He might have devoted to it a hundred or so pages of tender irony, enriched by complex and painstakingly ambiguous dialogues. The addition at the end of some melodramatic touch would not have been at all unlikely, nor would the essence of the tale have been changed by a different setting—London or Boston. The actual events took place in Buenos Aires, and there I shall leave them, limiting myself to a bare summary of the affair, since its slow evolution and sophisticated background are quite alien to my particular literary habits. To set down this story is for me a modest and peripheral adventure. I should warn my reader ahead of time that its episodes are of less importance than its characters and the relationship between them.

Clara Glencairn de Figueroa was stately and tall and had fiery red hair. Less intellectual than understanding, she was not witty, though she did appreciate the wit of others—

even of other women. Her mind was full of hospitality. Distinctions pleased her; perhaps that's why she traveled so much. She realized that her world was an all too arbitrary combination of rites and ceremonies, but these things amused her and she carried them out with dignity. Her family married her off very young to a distinguished lawyer, Isidro Figueroa, who was to become the Argentine ambassador to Canada and who ended by resigning that post, stating that in a time of telephones and telegraph, embassies were anachronisms and amounted to a needless public burden. This decision earned him the disapproval of all his colleagues; Clara liked the Ottawa climate—after all, she was of Scottish ancestry —and the duties of an ambassador's wife did not displease her, but she never once dreamed of protesting. Figueroa died soon after. Clara, following several years of indecision and self-searching, took up the exercise of painting—stimulated, perhaps, by the example of her friend Marta Pizarro.

It is characteristic of Marta Pizarro that when speaking about her, people referred to her as the sister of the brilliant Nélida Sara, who was married and divorced.

Before choosing palette and brush, Marta Pizarro had considered the alternative of writing. She could be quite clever in French, the language in which she had done most of her reading, while Spanish was to her—like Guaraní to ladies in the Province of Corrientes—little more than a household utensil. The literary supplements had placed within her reach pages of Lugones and of the Spaniard Ortega y Gasset; the style of these masters confirmed her suspicion that the language to which she had been born was less fit for expressing the mind or the passions than for verbal showing off. Of music, all she knew was what any person who attends a concert should know. Coming from the western province of San Luis, she began her career with faithful portraits of Juan Crisóstomo Lafinur and of Colonel Pascual Pringles, which were—as was to be expected—acquired by the Provincial Museum. From portraits of local worthies, she passed on to pictures of old houses in Buenos Aires, whose quiet patios she painted with quiet colors and not that stage-set showiness with which they are frequently endowed by others. Someone—surely not Clara Figueroa—remarked that her whole art drew its inspiration from the work of anonymous nineteenth-century Italian bricklayers. Between Clara Glencairn and Nélida Sara (who, according to gossip, had once had a fancy for Dr. Figueroa) there had always been a certain rivalry; perhaps the duel was between them, and Marta was merely a tool.

As is well known, most things originate in other countries and only in time find their way into the Argentine. That now so unjustly forgotten school of painters who call themselves concrete, or abstract, as if to show their utter scorn for logic and language, is but one of many examples. It was argued, as I recall, that just as music is expected to create its own world of sound, its sister art, painting, should be allowed to attempt a world of color and form without reference to any actual physical objects. The Dallas art critic Lee Kaplan wrote that this school's pictures, which outraged the bourgeoisie, followed the Biblical proscription, also shared by the Islamic world, that man shall make no images of living things. The iconoclasts, he argued, were going back to the true tradition of painting, which had been led astray by such heretics as Dürer and Rembrandt. Kaplan's enemies accused him of being influenced merely by broadloom rugs, kaleidoscopes, and men's neckwear.

All aesthetic revolutions put forth a temptation toward the irresponsible and the far too easy; Clara Glencairn chose to be an abstract painter. Having always been an admirer of Turner, she set as her goal the enrichment of abstract art with the diffused splendor of the Master. She worked under no pressure, painted over or destroyed a number of canvases, and in the winter of 1954 exhibited a series of temperas in a gallery on Suipacha Street whose specialty was paintings which, according to a military metaphor then in vogue, was called the vanguard. Something paradoxical happened. On the whole, the reviews were favorable, but the sect's official organ condemned her anomalous forms, which, although they were not representational, suggested the tumult of a sunset, a tangled forest, or the sea, and did not limit themselves to dots and stripes. Perhaps the first person to smile was Clara Glencairn. She had tried her best to be modern and the moderns had rejected her. The act of painting, however, mattered more to her than its public success, and she went on working. Indifferent to this episode, art also went on.

The secret duel had already begun. Marta was not only an artist; she was, as well, deeply committed to what may not unfairly be called the administrative side of art, and was assistant secretary of the organization known as the Giotto Circle. Sometime toward the middle of 1955, Marta managed to have Clara, who had already been accepted into the Circle, figure as a committee member among the Circle's new officers. The fact, in itself trivial, may be worth analyzing. Marta had lent support to her friend, but it is undeniable— although mysterious—that the person who confers a favor in some way stands above the one who receives it.

Around 1960, "two plastic artists of international stature" —may we be forgiven the jargon—were in the running for a first prize. One of the candidates, the elder, had dedicated solemn oils to the representation of awe-inspiring gauchos of a Scandinavian altitude; his rather young rival, a man in his early twenties, had won both praise and indignation through deliberate chaos. The members of the jury, all past fifty and fearing that the general public would impute outdated standards to them, tended to favor the latter painter, though deep down they rather disliked him. After arguing back and forth, at first politely and finally out of boredom, they could not reach an agreement. In the course of their third meeting, one of them remarked, "B. seems quite bad to me; really, I think he's even worse than Clara Figueroa."

"Would you give her your vote?" said another juror, with a trace of scorn.

"Yes," answered the first, at the brink of ill-temper.

That same evening, the prize was unanimously granted to Clara Glencairn. She was elegant, lovable, scandal had never touched her, and in her villa out in Pilar she gave parties to which the most lavish magazines sent photographers. The expected dinner in her honor was organized and offered by Marta. Clara thanked her with few and carefully chosen words, remarking that between the traditional and the new, or between order and adventure, no real opposition exists, and that what we now call tradition is made up of a centuries-old web of adventures. The banquet was attended by a large number of society people, by almost all the members of the jury, and by two or three painters.

All of us tend to think of our own circumstances in terms of a narrow range and to feel that other pastures are greener. The worship of the gaucho and the *Beatus ille* are but a wistfulness bred of city living; Clara Glencairn and Marta Pizarro, weary of the continual round of wealth and idleness, longed for the world of art, for people who had devoted their lives to the creation of things of beauty. My suspicion is that in Heaven the Blessed are of the opinion that the advantages of that locale have been overrated by theologians who were never actually there. Perhaps even in Hell the damned are not always satisfied.

A year or two later, in the city of Cartagena, there took place the First Congress of Inter-American Painting and Sculpture. Each country sent its representative. The themes of the conference—may we be forgiven the jargon—were of burning interest: Can the artist disregard the indigenous? Can he omit or slight flora and fauna? Can he be insensitive to problems of a social nature? Should he not join his voice to those suffering under the yoke of Saxon imperialism? Et cetera, et cetera. Before becoming ambassador to Canada, Dr. Figueroa had performed a diplomatic mission in Cartagena. Clara, a bit proud over the prize, would have liked returning there—this time as an artist. That hope was denied her; the government appointed Marta Pizarro. According to the impartial reports of correspondents from Buenos Aires, her participation (although not always persuasive) was on several occasions quite brilliant.

Life demands a passion. Both women found it in painting, or rather, in the relationship imposed on them by painting. Clara Glencairn painted against Marta and in a sense for Marta; each of them was her rival's judge and only public. In their pictures, which even then no one ever looked at, I think I observe—as was unavoidable—a mutual influence. Clara's sunset glows found their way into Marta Pizarro's patios, and Marta's fondness for straight lines simplified the ornateness of Clara's final stage. It is important to remember that the two women were genuinely fond of each other and that in the course of their intimate duel they behaved toward one another with perfect loyalty.

It was during those years that Marta, who by then was no longer so young, rejected a marriage proposal. All that interested her was her battle.

On the second of February, 1964, Clara Glencairn died of a heart ailment. The columns of the newspapers devoted long obituaries to her of the kind that are still quite common in the Argentine, where a woman is regarded as a member of the species, not an individual. Outside of some hasty mention of her dabbling in painting and of her impeccable good taste, she was praised for her religious devotion, her kindness, her constant and almost anonymous philanthropy, her illustrious family tree—General Glencairn had fought in the Brazilian campaign—and her outstanding place in society's highest circles. Marta realized that her life now lacked a meaning. She had never before felt so useless. Remembering her first endeavors, now so far in the past, she hung in the National Gallery a sober portrait of Clara after the manner of those English masters whom the two women had so admired. Some judged it her finest work. She was never to paint again.

In that delicate duel, only suspected by a few close friends, there were neither defeats nor victories nor even an open encounter, nor any visible circumstances other than those I have attempted respectfully to record. Only God (of whose aesthetic preferences we are unaware) can grant the final palm. The story that made its way in darkness ends in darkness.

The End of the Duel

The End of the Duel

It's a good many years ago now that Carlos Reyles, the son of the Uruguayan novelist, told me the story one summer evening out in Adrogué. In my memory, after all this time, the long chronicle of a feud and its grim ending are mixed up with the medicinal smell of the eucalyptus trees and the babbling voices of birds.

We sat talking, as usual, of the tangled history of our two countries, Uruguay and the Argentine. Reyles said that probably I'd heard of Juan Patricio Nolan, who had won quite a reputation as a brave man, a practical joker, and a rogue. Lying, I answered yes. Though Nolan had died back in the nineties, people still thought of him as a friend. As always happens, however, he had his enemies as well. Reyles gave me an account of one of Nolan's many pranks. The thing had happened a short time before the battle of Manantiales; two gauchos from Cerro Largo, Manuel Cardoso and Carmen Silveira, were the leading characters.

How and why did they begin hating each other? How, after a century, can one unearth the long-forgotten story of two men whose only claim to being remembered is their last duel? A foreman of Reyles' father, whose name was Laderecha and "who had the whiskers of a tiger," had collected from oral accounts certain details that I transcribe now with a good deal of misgiving, since both forgetfulness and memory are apt to be inventive.

Manuel Cardoso and Carmen Silveira had a few acres of land that bordered each other. Like the roots of other passions, those of hatred are mysterious, but there was talk of a quarrel over some unbranded cattle or a free-for-all horse race in which Silveira, who was the stronger of the two, had run Cardoso's horse off the edge of the course. Months afterward, a long two-handed game of *truco* of thirty points was to take place in the local saloon. Following almost every hand, Silveira congratulated his opponent on his skill, but in the end left him without a cent. When he tucked his winnings away in his money belt, Silveira thanked Cardoso for the lesson he had been given. It was then, I believe, that they were at the point of having it out. The game had had its ups and downs. In those rough places and in that day, man squared off against man and steel against steel. But the onlookers, who were quite a few, separated them. A peculiar twist of the story is that Manuel Cardoso and Carmen Silveira must have run across each other out in the hills on more than one occasion at sundown or at dawn, but they never actually faced each other until the very end. Maybe their poor and monotonous lives held nothing else for them than their hatred, and that was why they nursed it. In the long run, without suspecting it, each of the two became a slave to the other.

I no longer know whether the events I am about to relate are effects or causes. Cardoso, less out of love than out of boredom, took up with a neighbor girl, La Serviliana. That was all Silveira had to find out, and, after his manner, he began courting her and brought her to his shack. A few months later, finding her in the way, he threw her out. Full of spite, the woman tried to seek shelter at Cardoso's. Cardoso spent one night with her, and by the next noon packed her off. He did not want the other man's leavings.

It was around that same time, just before or just after La Serviliana, that the incident of Silveira's sheepdog took place. Silveira was very fond of the animal, and had named him Treinta y Tres, after Uruguay's thirty-three founding fathers. When the dog was found dead in a ditch, Silveira was quick to suspect who had given it poison.

Sometime during the winter of 1870, a civil war broke out between the Colorados, or Reds, who were in power, and Aparicio's Blancos, or Whites. The revolution found Silveira and Cardoso in the same crossroads saloon where they had played their game of cards. A Brazilian half-breed, at the head of a detachment of gaucho militiamen, harangued all those present, telling them that the country needed them and that the government oppression was unbearable. He handed around white badges to mark them as Blancos, and at the end of his speech, which nobody understood, everyone in the place was rounded up. They were not allowed even to say goodbye to their families.

Manuel Cardoso and Carmen Silveira accepted their fate; a soldier's life was no harder than a gaucho's. Sleeping in the open on their sheepskin saddle blankets was something to which they were already hardened, and as for killing men, that held no difficulty for hands already in the habit of killing cattle. The clinking of stirrups and weapons is one of the things always heard when cavalry enter into action. The man who is not wounded at the outset thinks himself invulnerable. A lack of imagination freed Cardoso and Silveira from fear and from pity, although once in a while, heading a charge, fear brushed them. They were never homesick. The idea of patriotism was alien to them, and, in spite of the badges they wore on their hats, one party was to them the same as the other. During the course of marches and countermarches, they learned what a man could do with a spear, and they found out that being companions allowed them to go on being enemies. They fought shoulder to shoulder and, for all we know, did not exchange a single word.

It was in the sultry fall of 1871 that their end was to come. The fight, which would not last an hour, happened in a place whose name they never knew. (Such places are later named by historians.) On the eve of battle, Cardoso crept on all fours into his officer's tent and asked him sheepishly would he save him one of the Reds if the Whites won the next day, because up till then he had not cut anyone's throat and he wanted to know what it was like. His superior promised him that if he handled himself like a man he would be granted that favor.

The Whites outnumbered the enemy, but the Reds were better equipped and cut them down from the crown of a hill. After two unsuccessful charges that never reached the summit, the Whites' commanding officer, badly wounded, surrendered. On the very spot, at his own request, he was put to death by the knife.

The men laid down their arms. Captain Juan Patricio Nolan, who commanded the Reds, arranged the expected execution of the prisoners down to the last detail. He was from Cerro Largo himself, and knew all about the old rivalry between Silveira and Cardoso. He sent for the pair and told them, "I already know you two can't stand the sight of each other, and that for some time now you've been looking for a chance to have it out. I have good news for you. Before sundown, the two of you are going to have that chance to show who's the better man. I'm going to stand you up and have your throats cut, and then you'll run a race. God knows who'll win." The soldier who had brought them took them away.

It was not long before the news spread throughout the camp. Nolan had made up his mind that the race would close the proceedings, but the prisoners sent him a representative to tell him that they, too, wanted to be spectators and to place wagers on the outcome. Nolan, who was an understanding man, let himself be convinced. The bets were laid down— money, riding gear, spears, sabers, and horses. In due time they would be handed over to the widows and next of kin. The heat was unusual. So that no one would miss his siesta, things were delayed until four o'clock. Nolan, in the South American style, kept them waiting another hour. He was probably discussing the campaign with his officers, his aide shuttling in and out with the maté kettle.

Both sides of the dirt road in front of the tents were lined with prisoners, who, to make things easier, squatted on the ground with their hands tied behind their backs. A few of them relieved their feelings in a torrent of swearwords, one went over and over the beginning of the Lord's Prayer, almost all were stunned. Of course, they could not smoke. They no longer cared about the race now, but they all watched.

"They'll be cutting my throat on me, too," one of them said, showing his envy.

"Sure, but along with the mob," said his neighbor.

"Same as you," the first man snapped back.

With his saber, a sergeant drew a line in the dust across the road. Silveira's and Cardoso's wrists had been untied so that they could run freely. A space of some five yards was between them. Each man toed the mark. A couple of the officers asked the two not to let them down because everyone had placed great faith in them, and the sums they had bet on them came to quite a pile.

It fell to Silveira's lot to draw as executioner the mulatto Nolan, whose forefathers had no doubt been slaves of the captain's family and therefore bore his name. Cardoso drew the Red's official cutthroat, a man from Corrientes well along in years, who, to comfort a condemned man, would pat him on the shoulder and tell him, "Take heart, friend. Women go through far worse when they give birth."

Their torsos bent forward, the two eager men did not look at each other. Nolan gave the signal.

The mulatto, swelling with pride to be at the center of attention, overdid his job and opened a showy slash that ran from ear to ear; the man from Corrientes did his with a narrow slit. Spurts of blood gushed from the men's throats. They dashed forward a number of steps before tumbling face down. Cardoso, as he fell, stretched out his arms. Perhaps never aware of it, he had won.

Rosendo's Tale

Rosendo's Tale

It was about eleven o'clock at night; I had entered the old grocery store–bar (which today is just a plain bar) at the corner of Bolívar and Venezuela. From off on one side, a man signaled me with a "psst." There must have been something forceful in his manner because I heeded him at once. He was seated at one of the small tables in front of an empty glass, and I somehow felt he had been sitting there for a long time. Neither short nor tall, he had the appearance of a common workingman or maybe an old farmhand. His thin moustache was graying. Fearful of his health, like most people in Buenos Aires, he had not taken off the scarf that draped his shoulders. He asked me to have a drink with him. I sat down and we chatted. All this took place sometime back in the early thirties. This is what the man told me.

———

You don't know me except maybe by reputation, but I know who you are. I'm Rosendo Juárez. The late Paredes must have told you about me. The old man could pull the wool over people's eyes and liked to stretch a point—not to cheat anybody, mind you, but just in fun. Well, seeing you and I have nothing better to do, I'm going to tell you exactly what happened that night. The night the Butcher got killed. You put all that down in a storybook, which I'm not equipped to pass judgment on, but I want you to know the truth about all that trumped-up stuff.

Things happen to you and it's only years later you begin understanding them. What happened to me that night really had its start a long time back. I grew up in the neighborhood of the Maldonado, way out past Floresta. The Maldonado was just a ditch then, a kind of sewer, and it's a good thing they've covered it over now. I've always been of the opinion that the march of progress can't be held back—not by anybody. Anyway, a man's born where he's born. It never entered my head to find out who my father was. Clementina Juárez—that was my mother—was a decent woman who earned a living doing laundry. As far as I know, she was from Entre Ríos or Uruguay; anyhow, she always talked about her relatives from Concepción del Uruguay. I grew up like a weed. I first learned to handle a knife the way everyone else did, fencing with a charred stick. If you jabbed your man, it left a mark. Soccer hadn't taken us over yet—it was still in the hands of the English.

One night at the corner bar, a young guy named Garmendia began taunting me, trying to pick a fight. I played deaf, but this other guy, who'd had a few, kept it up. We stepped out. Then from the sidewalk he swung open the door and said back inside to the people, "Don't anybody worry, I'll be right back."

I somehow got hold of a knife. We went off toward the brook, slow, our eyes on each other. He had a few years on me. We'd played at that fencing game a number of times together, and I had the feeling he was going to cut me up in ribbons. I went down the right-hand side of the road and he went down the left. He stumbled on some dry clods of mud. That moment was all I needed. I got the jump on him, almost without thinking, and opened a slice in his face. We got locked in a clinch, there was a minute when anything might have happened, and in the end I got my knife in and it was all over. Only later on did I find out I'd been cut up, too. But only a few scratches. That night I saw how easy it was to kill a man or to get killed. The water in the brook was pretty low; stalling for time, I half hid him behind one of the brick kilns. Fool that I was, I went and slipped off that fancy ring of his that he always wore with the nice stone in it. I put it on, I straightened my hat, and I went back to the bar. I walked in nonchalant, saying to them, "Looks like the one who came back was me."

I asked for a shot of rum and, to tell the truth, I needed it bad. It was then somebody noticed the blood on my sleeve.

I spent that whole night tossing and turning on my cot, and it was almost light outside before I dropped off and slept. Late the next day two cops came looking for me. My mother (may she rest in peace) began shrieking. They herded me along just like I was some kind of criminal. Two nights and two days I had to wait there in the cooler. Nobody came to see me, either, outside of Luis Irala—a real friend—only they wouldn't let him in. Then the third morning the police captain sent for me. He sat there in his chair, not even looking at me, and said, "So you're the one who took care of Garmendia, are you?"

"If that's what you say," I answered.

"You call me *sir*. And don't get funny or try beating around the bush. Here are the sworn statements of witnesses and the ring that was found in your house. Just sign this confession and get it over with."

He dipped the pen in the inkwell and handed it to me.

"Let me do some thinking, Captain sir," I came out with.

"I'll give you twenty-four hours where you can do some hard thinking—in the cooler. I'm not going to rush you. If you don't care to see reason, you can get used to the idea of a little vacation up on Las Heras—the penitentiary."

As you can probably imagine, I didn't understand.

"Look," he said, "if you come around, all you'll get is a few days. Then I'll let you go, and don Nicolás Paredes has already given me his word he'll straighten things out for you."

Actually, it was ten days. Then at last they remembered me. I signed what they wanted, and one of the two cops took me around to Paredes' house on Cabrera Street.

Horses were tied to the hitching post, and in the entrance-way and inside the place there were more people than around a whorehouse. It looked to me like the party headquarters. Don Nicolás, who was sipping his maté, finally got around to me. Taking his good time, he told me he was sending me out to Morón, where they were getting ready for the elections. He was putting me in touch with Mr. Laferrer, who would try me out. He had the letter written by some kid all dressed in black, who, from what I heard, made up poems about tenements and filth—stuff that no refined public would dream of reading. I thanked Paredes for the favor and left. When I got to the corner, the cop wasn't tailing me any more.

Providence knows what it's up to; everything had turned out for the best. Garmendia's death, which at first had caused me a lot of worry, now opened things up for me. Of course, the law had me in the palm of their hands. If I was no use to the party they'd clap me back inside, but I felt pretty good and was counting on myself.

Mr. Laferrer warned me I was going to have to walk the straight and narrow with him, and said if I did I might even become his bodyguard. I came through with what was expected of me. In Morón, and later on in my part of town, I earned the trust of my bosses. The cops and the party kept on building up my reputation as a tough guy. I turned out to be pretty good at organizing the vote around the polls here in the capital and out in the province. I won't take up your time going into details about brawls and bloodletting, but let me tell you, in those days elections were lively affairs. I could never stand the Radicals, who down to this day are still hanging onto the beard of their chief Alem. There wasn't a soul around who didn't hold me in respect. I got hold of a woman, La Lujanera, and a fine-looking sorrel. For years I tried to live up to the part of the outlaw Moreira, who, in his time —the way I figure it—was probably trying to play the part of some other gaucho outlaw. I took to cards and absinthe.

An old man has a way of rambling on and on, but now I'm coming to the part I want you to hear. I wonder if I've already mentioned Luis Irala. The kind of friend you don't find every day. Irala was a man already well along in years. He never was afraid of work, and he took a liking to me. In his whole life he never had anything to do with politics. He was a carpenter by trade. He never caused anyone trouble and never allowed anyone to cause him trouble. One morning he came to see me and he said, "Of course, you've heard by now that Casilda's left me. Rufino Aguilera took her away from me."

I'd known that customer around Morón. I answered, "Yes, I know all about him. Of all the Aguileras, he's the least rotten."

"Rotten or not, now he'll have to reckon with me."

I thought that over for a while and told him, "Nobody takes anything away from anybody. If Casilda left you, it's because she cares for Rufino and you mean nothing to her."

"And what are people going to say? That I'm a coward?"

"My advice is don't get yourself mixed up in gossip about what people might say or about a woman who has no use for you."

"It's not her I'm worried about. A man who thinks five minutes straight about a woman is no man, he's a queer. Casilda has no heart. The last night we spent together she told me I wasn't as young as I used to be."

"Maybe she was telling you the truth."

"That's what hurts. What matters to me now is Rufino."

"Be careful there. I've seen Rufino in action around the polls in Merlo. He's a flash with a knife."

"You think I'm afraid of him?"

"I know you're not afraid of him, but think it over. One of two things—if you kill him, you get put away; if he kills you, you go six feet under."

"Maybe so. What would you do in my shoes?"

"I don't know, but my own life isn't exactly a model. I'm only a guy who became a party strong-arm man trying to beat a jail sentence."

"I'm not going to be the strong-arm guy for any party, I'm only out to settle a debt."

"So you're going to risk your peace and quiet for a man you don't know and a woman you don't love any more?"

He wouldn't hear me out. He just left. The next day the news came that he challenged Rufino in a saloon in Morón, and Rufino killed him. He was out to kill, and he got killed —but a fair fight, man to man. I'd given him my honest advice as a friend, but somehow I felt guilty just the same.

A few days after the wake, I went to a cockfight. I'd never been very big on cockfights, and that Sunday, to tell the truth, I had all I could do to stomach the thing. What is it in these animals, I kept thinking, that makes them gouge each other's eyes like that?

The night of my story, the night of the end of my story, I

had told the boys I'd show up at Blackie's for the dance. So many years ago now, and that dress with the flowers my woman was wearing still comes back to me. The party was out in the backyard. Of course, there was the usual drunk or two trying to raise hell, but I took good care to see that things went off the way they ought to. It wasn't twelve yet when these strangers put in an appearance. One of them—the one they called the Butcher and who got himself stabbed in the back that same night—stood us all to a round of drinks. The odd thing was that the two of us looked a lot alike. Something was in the air; he drew up to me and began praising me up and down. He said he was from the Northside, where he'd heard a thing or two about me. I let him go on, but I was already sizing him up. He wasn't letting the gin alone, either, maybe to work up his courage, and finally he came out and asked me to fight. Then something happened that nobody ever understood. In that big loudmouth I saw myself, the same as in a mirror, and it made me feel ashamed. I wasn't scared; maybe if I'd been scared I'd have fought with him. I just stood there as if nothing happened. This other guy, with his face just inches away from mine, began shouting so everyone could hear, "The trouble is you're nothing but a coward."

"Maybe so," I said. "I'm not afraid of being taken for a coward. If it makes you feel good, why don't you say you've called me a son of a bitch, too, and that I've let you spit all over me. Now—are you any happier?"

La Lujanera took out the knife I always carried in my vest lining and, burning up inside, she shoved it into my hand. To clinch it, she said, "Rosendo, I think you're going to need this."

I let it drop and walked out, but not hurrying. The boys made way for me. They were stunned. What did it matter to me what they thought.

To make a clean break with that life, I took off for Uruguay, where I found myself work as a teamster. Since coming back to Buenos Aires, I've settled around here. San Telmo always was a respectable neighborhood.

The Intruder

The Intruder

. . . passing the love of women.
              2 Samuel 1:26

People say (but this is unlikely) that the story was first told
by Eduardo, the younger of the Nelsons, at the wake of his
elder brother Cristián, who died in his sleep sometime back in
the nineties out in the district of Morón. The fact is that
someone got it from someone else during the course of that
drawn-out and now dim night, between one sip of maté and
the next, and told it to Santiago Dabove, from whom I heard
it. Years later, in Turdera, where the story had taken place, I
heard it again. The second and more elaborate version closely
followed the one Santiago told, with the usual minor variations and discrepancies. I set down the story now because I
see in it, if I'm not mistaken, a brief and tragic mirror of the
character of those hard-bitten men living on the edge of Buenos Aires before the turn of the century. I hope to do this in
a straightforward way, but I see in advance that I shall give in
to the writer's temptation of emphasizing or adding certain
details.

In Turdera, where they lived, they were called the Nilsens.
The priest there told me that his predecessor remembered

having seen in the house of these people—somewhat in amazement—a worn Bible with a dark binding and black-letter type; on the back flyleaf he caught a glimpse of names and dates written in by hand. It was the only book in the house—the roaming chronicle of the Nilsens, lost as one day all things will be lost. The rambling old house, which no longer stands, was of unplastered brick; through the arched entranceway you could make out a patio paved with red tiles and beyond it a second one of hard-packed earth. Few people, at any rate, ever set foot inside; the Nilsens kept to themselves. In their almost bare rooms they slept on cots. Their extravagances were horses, silver-trimmed riding gear, the short-bladed dagger, and getting dressed up on Saturday nights, when they blew their money freely and got themselves into boozy brawls. They were both tall, I know, and wore their red hair long. Denmark or Ireland, which they probably never heard of, ran in the blood of these two Argentine brothers. The neighborhood feared the Redheads; it is likely that one of them, at least, had killed his man. Once, shoulder to shoulder, they tangled with the police. It is said that the younger brother was in a fight with Juan Iberra in which he didn't do too badly, and that, according to those in the know, is saying something. They were drovers, teamsters, horse thieves, and, once in a while, professional gamblers. They had a reputation for stinginess, except when drink and cardplaying turned them into spenders. Of their relatives or where they themselves came from, nothing is known. They owned a cart and a yoke of oxen.

Their physical make-up differed from that of the rest of the toughs who gave the Costa Brava its unsavory reputation. This, and a lot that we don't know, helps us understand the close ties between them. To fall out with one of them was to reckon with two enemies.

The Nilsens liked carousing with women, but up until then

their amorous escapades had always been carried out in darkened passageways or in whorehouses. There was no end of talk, then, when Cristián brought Juliana Burgos to live with him. Admittedly, in this way he gained a servant, but it is also true that he took to squandering his money buying her the most hideous junk jewelry, and showing her off at parties. At those dingy parties held in tenements, where suggestive dance steps were strictly forbidden and where, at that time, partners still danced with a good six inches of light showing between them. Juliana was a dark girl and her eyes had a slight slant to them; all anyone had to do was look at her and she'd break into a smile. For a poor neighborhood, where drudgery and neglect wear women out, she was not bad-looking.

In the beginning, Eduardo went places with them. Later, at one point, he set out on a journey north to Arrecifes on some business or other, returning home with a girl he had picked up along the way. But after a few days he threw her out. He turned more sullen; he took to drinking alone at the corner saloon and kept completely to himself. He had fallen in love with Cristián's woman. The whole neighborhood, which may have realized it before he did, maliciously and cheerfully looked forward to the enmity about to break out between the two brothers.

Late one night, on coming home from the corner, Eduardo saw Cristián's horse, a big bay, tied to the hitching post. Inside in the patio, dressed in his Sunday best, his older brother was waiting for him. The woman shuttled in and out serving maté. Cristián said to Eduardo, "I'm on my way over to Farías' place, where they're throwing a party. Juliana stays here with you; if you want her, use her."

His tone was half commanding, half friendly. Eduardo stood there a while staring at him, not knowing what to do. Cristián got up, said goodbye—to his brother, not to Juliana, who was no more than an object—mounted his horse, and rode off at a jog, casually.

From that night on they shared her. Nobody will ever know the details of this strange partnership which outraged even the Costa Brava's sense of decency. The arrangement went well for several weeks, but it could not last. Between them the brothers never mentioned her name, not even to call her, but they kept looking for, and finding, reasons to be at odds. They argued over the sale of some hides, but what they were really arguing about was something else. Cristián took to raising his voice, while Eduardo kept silent. Without knowing it, they were watching each other. In tough neighborhoods a man never admits to anyone—not even to himself—that a woman matters beyond lust and possession, but the two brothers were in love. This, in some way, made them feel ashamed.

One afternoon, in the square in Lomas, Eduardo ran into Juan Iberra, who congratulated him on this beauty he'd got hold of. It was then, I believe, that Eduardo let him have it. Nobody—not to *his* face—was going to poke fun at Cristián.

The woman attended both men's wants with an animal submission, but she was unable to keep hidden a certain preference, probably for the younger man, who had not refused sharing her but who had not proposed it either.

One day, they ordered Juliana to bring two chairs out into the first patio and then not show her face for a while because they had things to talk over. Expecting a long session between them, she lay down for a nap, but before very long they woke her up. She was to fill a sack with all her belongings, including her glass-bead rosary and the tiny crucifix her mother had left her. Without any explanation, they lifted her onto the oxcart and set out on a long, tiresome, and silent journey. It had rained; the roads were heavy with mud, and it was nearly daybreak before they reached Morón. There they sold her to the woman who ran the whorehouse. The terms had already been agreed to; Cristián pocketed the money and later on split it with his brother.

Back in Turdera, the Nilsens, up till then trapped in the web (which was also a routine) of this monstrous love affair, tried to take up their old life of men among men. They went back to cardplaying, to cockfights, to their Saturday night binges. At times, perhaps, they felt they were saved, but they often indulged—each on his own—in unaccountable or only too accountable absences. A little before the year was out, the younger brother said he had business in the city. Immediately, Cristián went off to Morón; at the hitching post of the whorehouse he recognized Eduardo's piebald. Cristián walked in; there was his brother, sure enough, waiting his turn. It is said that Cristián told him, "If we go on this way, we'll wear out the horses. We'd be better off keeping her close at hand."

He spoke with the owner of the place, drew a handful of coins out of his money belt, and they took the girl away. Juliana rode with Cristián. Eduardo dug his spurs into his horse, not wanting to see them together.

They went back to what has already been told. Their solution had ended in failure, for the two had fallen into cheating. Cain was on the loose here, but the affection between the Nilsens was great—who knows what hard times and what dangers they may have faced together!—and they preferred taking their feelings out on others. On strangers, on the dogs, on Juliana, who had set this wedge between them.

The month of March was coming to a close and there was no sign of the heat's letting up. One Sunday (on Sundays people go to bed early), Eduardo, on his way home from the corner saloon, saw that Cristián was yoking the oxen. Cristián said to him, "Come on. We have to leave some hides off at

Pardo's place. I've already loaded them; let's make the best of the night air."

Pardo's warehouse lay, I believe, farther south; they took the old cattle trail, then turned down a side road. As night fell, the countryside seemed wider and wider.

They skirted a growth of tall reeds; Cristián threw down the cigar he had just lit, and said evenly, "Let's get busy, brother. In a while the buzzards will take over. This afternoon I killed her. Let her stay here with all her trinkets, she won't cause us any more harm."

They threw their arms around each other, on the verge of tears. One more link bound them now—the woman they had cruelly sacrificed and their common need to forget her.

The Meeting

To Susana Bombal

The Meeting

Anyone leafing his way through the morning paper does so
either to escape his surroundings or to provide himself with
small talk for later in the day, so it is not to be wondered at
that no one any longer remembers—or else remembers as
in a dream—the famous and once widely discussed case of
Maneco Uriarte and of Duncan. The event took place, furthermore, back around 1910, the year of the comet and the
Centennial, and since then we have had and have lost so
many things. Both protagonists are now dead; those who witnessed the episode solemnly swore silence. I, too, raised my
hand for the oath, feeling the importance of the ritual with all
the romantic seriousness of my nine or ten years. I do not
know whether the others noticed that I had given my word;
I do not know whether they kept theirs. Anyway, here is the
story, with all the inevitable variations brought about by time
and by good or bad writing.

My cousin Lafinur took me to a barbecue that evening at a
country house called The Laurels, which belonged to some
friends of his. I cannot fix its exact location; let us take any of
those suburban towns lying just to the north, shaded and

quiet, that slope down to the river and that have nothing in common with sprawling Buenos Aires and its surrounding prairie. The journey by train lasted long enough to seem endless to me, but time for children—as is well known—flows slowly. It was already dark when we passed through the villa's main gate. Here, I felt, were all the ancient, elemental things: the smell of meat cooking golden brown, the trees, the dogs, the kindling wood, and the fire that brings men together.

The guests numbered about a dozen; all were grown-ups. The eldest, I learned later, was not yet thirty. They were also—this I was soon to find out—well versed in matters about which I am still somewhat backward: race horses, the right tailors, motorcars, and notoriously expensive women. No one ruffled my shyness, no one paid any attention to me. The lamb, slowly and skillfully prepared by one of the hired men, kept us a long time in the big dining room. The dates of vintages were argued back and forth. There was a guitar; my cousin, if I remember correctly, sang a couple of Elías Regules' ballads about gauchos in the back country of Uruguay and some verses in dialect, in the incipient *lunfardo* of those days, about a knife fight in a brothel on Junín Street. Coffee and Havana cigars were brought in. Not a word about getting back. I felt (in the words of the poet Lugones) the fear of what is suddenly too late. I dared not look at the clock. In order to disguise my boyish loneliness among grown-ups, I put away—not really liking it—a glass or two of wine. Uriarte, in a loud voice, proposed to Duncan a two-handed game of poker. Someone objected that that kind of play made for a poor game and suggested a hand of four. Duncan agreed, but Uriarte, with a stubbornness that I did not understand and that I did not try to understand, insisted on the first scheme. Outside of *truco*—a game whose real aim is to pass time with mischief and verses—and of the modest mazes of solitaire, I never enjoyed cards. I slipped away without anyone's noticing. A rambling old house, unfamiliar and dark (only in the dining room was there light), means more to a boy than a new country means to a traveler. Step by step, I explored the rooms; I recall a billiard room, a long gallery with rectangular and diamond-shaped panes, a couple of rocking chairs, and a window from which you could just make out a summerhouse. In the darkness I lost my way; the owner of the house, whose name, as I recall after all these years, may have been Acevedo or Acebal, finally came across me somehow. Out of kindness or perhaps out of a collector's vanity, he led me to a display cabinet. On lighting a lamp, I saw the glint of steel. It was a collection of knives that had once been in the hands of famous fighters. He told me that he had a bit of land somewhere to the north around Pergamino, and that he had been picking up these things on his travels back and forth across the province. He opened the cabinet and, without looking at what was written on the tags, he began giving me accounts of each item; they were more or less the same except for dates and place names. I asked him whether among the weapons he might have the dagger of Juan Moreira, who was in that day the archetype of the gaucho, as later Martín Fierro and Don Segundo Sombra would be. He had to confess that he hadn't but that he could show me one like it, with a U-shaped crosspiece in the hilt. He was interrupted by the sound of angry voices. At once he shut the cabinet and turned to leave; I followed him.

Uriarte was shouting that his opponent had tried to cheat him. All the others stood around the two players. Duncan, I remember, was a taller man than the rest of the company, and was well built, though somewhat round-shouldered; his face was expressionless, and his hair was so light it was almost white. Maneco Uriarte was nervous, dark, with perhaps a touch of Indian blood, and wore a skimpy, petulant moustache. It was obvious that everybody was drunk; I do not know whether there were two or three emptied bottles on the floor or whether an excess of movies suggests this false memory to me. Uriarte's insults did not let up; at first sharp, they now grew obscene. Duncan appeared not to hear, but finally, as though weary, he got up and threw a punch. From the floor, Uriarte snarled that he was not going to take this outrage, and he challenged Duncan to fight.

Duncan said no, and added, as though to explain, "The trouble is I'm afraid of you."

Everybody howled with laughter.

Uriarte, picking himself up, answered, "I'm going to have it out with you, and right now."

Someone—may he be forgiven for it—remarked that weapons were not lacking.

I do not know who went and opened the glass cabinet. Maneco Uriarte picked out the showiest and longest dagger, the one with the U-shaped crosspiece; Duncan, almost absentmindedly, picked a wooden-handled knife with the stamp of a tiny tree on the blade. Someone else said it was just like Maneco to play it safe, to choose a sword. It astonished no one that his hand began shaking; what was astonishing is that the same thing happened with Duncan.

Tradition demands that men about to fight should respect the house in which they are guests, and step outside. Half on a spree, half seriously, we all went out into the damp night. I was not drunk—at least, not on wine—but I was reeling with adventure; I wished very hard that someone would be killed, so that later I could tell about it and always remember it. Maybe at that moment the others were no more adult than I was. I also had the feeling that an overpowering current was dragging us on and would drown us. Nobody believed the least bit in Maneco's accusation; everyone saw it as the fruit of an old rivalry, exacerbated by the wine.

We pushed our way through a clump of trees, leaving behind the summerhouse. Uriarte and Duncan led the way, wary of each other. The rest of us strung ourselves out around the edge of an opening of lawn. Duncan had stopped there in the moonlight and said, with mild authority, "This looks like the right place."

The two men stood in the center, not quite knowing what to do. A voice rang out: "Let go of all that hardware and use your hands!"

But the men were already fighting. They began clumsily, almost as if they were afraid of hurting each other; they began by watching the blades, but later their eyes were on one another. Uriarte had laid aside his anger, Duncan his contempt or aloofness. Danger, in some way, had transfigured them; these were now two men fighting, not boys. I had imagined the fight as a chaos of steel; instead, I was able to follow it, or almost follow it, as though it were a game of chess. The intervening years may, of course, have exaggerated or blurred what I saw. I do not know how long it lasted; there are events that fall outside the common measure of time.

Without ponchos to act as shields, they used their forearms to block each lunge of the knife. Their sleeves, soon hanging in shreds, grew black with blood. I thought that we had gone wrong in supposing that they knew nothing about this kind of fencing. I noticed right off that they handled themselves in different ways. Their weapons were unequal. Duncan, in order to make up for his disadvantage, tried to stay in close to the other man; Uriarte kept stepping back to be able to lunge out with long, low thrusts. The same voice that had called attention to the display cabinet shouted out now: "They're killing each other! Stop them!"

But no one dared break it up. Uriarte had lost ground; Duncan charged him. They were almost body to body now.

Uriarte's weapon sought Duncan's face. Suddenly the blade seemed shorter, for it was piercing the taller man's chest. Duncan lay stretched out on the grass. It was at this point that he said, his voice very low, "How strange. All this is like a dream."

He did not shut his eyes, he did not move, and I had seen a man kill another man.

Maneco Uriarte bent over the body, sobbing openly, and begged to be forgiven. The thing he had just done was beyond him. I know now that he regretted less having committed a crime than having carried out a senseless act.

I did not want to look anymore. What I had wished for so much had happened, and it left me shaken. Lafinur told me later that they had had to struggle hard to pull out the weapon. A makeshift council was formed. They decided to lie as little as possible and to elevate this duel with knives to a duel with swords. Four of them volunteered as seconds, among them Acebal. In Buenos Aires anything can be fixed; someone always has a friend.

On top of the mahogany table where the men had been playing, a pack of English cards and a pile of bills lay in a jumble that nobody wanted to look at or to touch.

In the years that followed, I often considered revealing the story to some friend, but always I felt that there was a greater pleasure in being the keeper of a secret than in telling it. However, around 1929, a chance conversation suddenly moved me one day to break my long silence. The retired police captain, don José Olave, was recalling stories about men from the tough riverside neighborhood of the Retiro who had been handy with their knives; he remarked that when they were out to kill their man, scum of this kind had no use for the rules of the game, and that before all the fancy playing with daggers that you saw now on the stage, knife fights were few and far between. I said I had witnessed one, and gave him an account of what had happened nearly twenty years earlier.

He listened to me with professional attention, then said, "Are you sure Uriarte and What's-His-Name never handled a knife before? Maybe they had picked up a thing or two around their fathers' ranches."

"I don't think so," I said. "Everybody there that night knew one another pretty well, and I can tell you they were all amazed at the way the two men fought."

Olave went on in his quiet manner, as if thinking aloud. "One of the weapons had a U-shaped crosspiece in the handle. There were two daggers of that kind which became quite famous—Moreira's and Juan Almada's. Almada was from down south, in Tapalquén."

Something seemed to come awake in my memory. Olave continued. "You also mentioned a knife with a wooden handle, one with the Little Tree brand. There are thousands of them, but there was one—"

He broke off for a moment, then said, "Señor Acevedo had a big property up around Pergamino. There was another of these famous toughs from up that way—Juan Almanza was his name. This was along about the turn of the century. When he was fourteen, he killed his first man with one of these knives. From then on, for luck, he stuck to the same one. Juan Almanza and Juan Almada had it in for each other, jealous of the fact that many people confused the two. For a long time they searched high and low for one another, but they never met. Juan Almanza was killed by a stray bullet during some election brawl or other. The other man, I think, died a natural death in a hospital bed in Las Flores."

Nothing more was said. Each of us was left with his own conclusions.

Nine or ten men, none of whom is any longer living, saw what my eyes saw—that sudden stab and the body under the night sky—but perhaps what we were really seeing was the end of another story, an older story. I began to wonder whether it was Maneco Uriarte who killed Duncan or whether in some uncanny way it could have been the weapons, not the men, which fought. I still remember how Uriarte's hand shook when he first gripped his knife, and the same with Duncan, as though the knives were coming awake after a long sleep side by side in the cabinet. Even after their gauchos were dust, the knives—the knives, not their tools, the men—knew how to fight. And that night they fought well.

Things last longer than people; who knows whether these knives will meet again, who knows whether the story ends here.

Juan Muraña

Juan Muraña

For years now, I have been telling people I grew up in that part of Buenos Aires known as Palermo. This, I've come to realize, is mere literary bravado; the truth is that I really grew up on the inside of a long iron picket fence in a house with a garden and with my father's and his father's library. The Palermo of knife fights and of guitar playing lurked (so they say) on street corners and down back alleys. In 1930, I wrote a study of Evaristo Carriego, a neighbor of ours, a poet and glorifier of the city's outlying slums. A little after that, chance brought me face to face with Emilio Trápani. I was on the train to Morón. Trápani, who was sitting next to the window, called me by name. For some time I could not place him, so many years had passed since we'd been classmates in a school on Thames Street. Roberto Godel, another classmate, may remember him.

Trápani and I never had any great liking for each other. Time had set us apart, and also our mutual indifference. He had taught me, I now recall, all the basic slang words of the day. Riding along, we struck up one of those trivial conversations that force you to unearth pointless facts and that lead up to the discovery of the death of a fellow-schoolmate who is no longer anything more than a name. Then, abruptly, Trápani said to me, "Someone lent me your Carriego book, where you're talking about hoodlums all the time. Tell me, Borges, what in the world can you know about hoodlums?" He stared at me with a kind of wonder.

"I've done research," I answered.

Not letting me go on, he said, "Research is the word, all right. Personally, I have no use for research—I know these people inside out." After a moment's silence, he added, as though he were letting me in on a secret, "I'm Juan Muraña's nephew."

Of all the men around Palermo famous for handling a knife way back in the nineties, the one with the widest reputation was Muraña. Trápani went on, "Florentina—my aunt—was his wife. Maybe you'll be interested in this story."

Certain devices of a literary nature and one or two longish sentences led me to suspect that this was not the first time he had told the story.

My mother [Trápani said] could never quite stomach the fact that her sister had linked herself up with a man like Muraña, who to her was just a big brute, while to Aunt Florentina he was a man of action. A lot of stories circulated about my uncle's end. Some say that one night when he was dead drunk he tumbled from the seat of his wagon, making the turn around the corner of Coronel, and cracked his skull on the cobblestones. It's also said that the law was on his heels and he ran away to Uruguay. My mother, who couldn't stand her brother-in-law, never explained to me what actually happened. I was just a small boy then and have no memories of him.

Along about the time of the Centennial, we were living in a long, narrow house on Russell Alley. The back door, which was always kept locked, opened on the other side of the block, on San Salvador Street. My aunt, who was well along in years and a bit queer, had a room with us up in our attic. Big-boned but thin as a stick, she was—or seemed to me —very tall. She also wasted few words. Living in fear of fresh air, she never went out; nor did she like our going into her room. More than once, I caught her stealing and hiding food. The talk around the neighborhood was that Muraña's death, or disappearance, had affected her mind. I remember her always in black. She had also fallen into the habit of talking to herself.

Our house belonged to a certain Mr. Luchessi, the owner of a barbershop on the Southside, in Barracas. My mother, who did piecework at home as a seamstress, was in financial straits. Without being able to understand them, I heard whispered terms like "court order" and "eviction notice." My mother was really at her wit's end, and my aunt kept saying stubbornly that Juan was not going to stand by and let the gringo, that wop, throw us out. She recalled the incident— which all of us knew by heart—of a big-mouthed tough from the Southside who had dared doubt her husband's courage. Muraña, the moment he found out, took all the trouble to go clear across the town, ferret the man out, put him straight with a blow of his knife, and dump his body into the Riachuelo. I don't know if the story's true; what matters is that it was told and that it became accepted.

I saw myself sleeping in empty lots on Serrano Street or begging handouts or going around with a basket of peaches. Selling on the streets tempted me, because it would free me from school. I don't know how long our troubles lasted. Your late father once told us that you can't measure time by days, the way you measure money by dollars and cents, because dollars are all the same while every day is different and maybe every hour as well. I didn't quite understand what he meant, but the words stuck in my mind.

One night, I had a dream that ended in a nightmare. I dreamed of my Uncle Juan. I had never got to know him, but I thought of him as a burly man with a touch of the Indian about him, a sparse moustache and his hair long. He and I were heading south, cutting through huge stone quarries and scrub, but these quarries and thickets were also Thames Street. In the dream, the sun was high overhead. Uncle Juan was dressed in a black suit. He stopped beside a sort of scaffolding in a narrow mountain pass. He held his hand under his jacket, around the level of his heart—not like a person who's about to pull a knife but as though he were keeping the hand hidden. In a very sad voice, he told me, "I've changed a lot." He withdrew the hand, and what I saw was the claw of a vulture. I woke up screaming in the dark.

The next day, my mother made me go with her to Luchessi's. I know she was going to ask him for extra time; she probably took me along so that our landlord would see her helplessness. She didn't mention a word of this to her sister, who would never have let her lower herself in such a way. I hadn't ever set foot in Barracas before; it seemed to me there were a lot more people around than I imagined there'd be, and a lot more traffic and fewer vacant lots. From the corner, we saw several policemen and a flock of people in front of the house we were looking for. A neighbor went from group to group telling everyone that around three o'clock that morning he had been awakened by someone thumping on a door. He heard the door open and someone go in. Nobody shut the door, and as soon as it was light Luchessi was found lying there in the entranceway, half dressed. He'd been stabbed a number of times. The man lived alone; the authorities never caught up with the murderer. Nothing, it seems, had been stolen. At the time, somebody recalled that the deceased had almost lost his sight. In an important-sounding voice, someone else said, "His time had come." This judgment and the tone made an impression on me; as the years passed I was to find out that any time a person dies there's always somebody who makes this same discovery.

At the wake, we were offered coffee and I had a cup. In the coffin there was a wax dummy in place of the dead man. I mentioned this to my mother; one of the undertaker's men laughed and explained to me that the dummy dressed in black was Mr. Luchessi. I stood spellbound, staring at him. My mother had to yank me away.

For months afterward, nobody talked of anything else. Crimes were so few in those days; just remember all the fuss that was made over the case of Melena, Campana, and Silletero. The one person in all Buenos Aires who showed no interest whatever was Aunt Florentina. She kept on saying, with the persistence of old age, "I told you Juan would never let that gringo put us out in the street."

One day, it rained buckets. As I could not go to school that morning, I began rummaging through the house. I climbed up to the attic. There was my aunt, sitting with her hands folded together; I could tell that she wasn't even thinking. The room smelled damp. In one corner stood the iron bedstead, with her rosary beads attached to one of the bars, in another a wooden chest where she kept her clothes. A picture of the Virgin was pinned to one of the whitewashed walls. On the table by the bed was a candlestick. Without lifting her eyes, my aunt said, "I know what brings you up here. Your mother sent you. She just doesn't seem to understand that it was Juan who saved us."

"Juan?" I said, amazed. "Juan died over ten years ago."

"Juan is here," she told me. "Do you want to see him?" She opened the drawer of the night table and took out a dagger, then went on speaking in a soft, low voice. "Here he is. I knew he would never forsake me. In the whole world there hasn't been another man like him. He didn't let the gringo get out a word."

It was only then that I understood. That poor raving woman had murdered Luchessi. Driven by hate, by madness, and maybe—who knows—by love, she had slipped out by the back door, had made her way block after block in the dead of night, had found the house she was after, and, with those big, bony hands, had sunk the dagger. The dagger was Muraña—it was the dead man she had gone on worshiping.

I never knew whether she told my mother the story or not. She died a short time before the eviction.

Here Trápani—whom I have never run across again—ended his account. Since then, I have often thought about this bereft woman and about her man. Juan Muraña walked the familiar streets of my boyhood; I may have seen him many times, unawares. He was a man who knew what all men come to know, a man who tasted death and was afterward a knife, and is now the memory of a knife, and will tomorrow be oblivion—the oblivion that awaits us all.

The Elder Lady

The Elder Lady

On the fourteenth of January, 1941, María Justina Rubio de Jáuregui was to be one hundred years old. She was the last surviving daughter of any of the soldiers who had fought in the South American War of Independence.

Colonel Mariano Rubio, her father, was what might, without irreverence, be called a minor immortal. Born in 1799 in the Buenos Aires parish of La Merced, the son of local land-owners, he was promoted to ensign in San Martín's Army of the Andes, and he fought in the battle of Chacabuco, in the defeat of Cancha Rayada, at Maipú, and, two years after that, at Arequipa. It is told that on the eve of one of these battles, he and a fellow-officer, José de Olavarría, exchanged swords. At the beginning of April, 1823, there took place the famous engagement of Big Hill, which, having been fought in a valley between two summits, is often also known as the battle of Red Hill. Always envious of our glories, the Venezuelans attribute this victory to General Simón Bolívar, but the impartial observer, the Argentine historian, is not easily taken in and knows only too well that the laurels rightfully belong to

Colonel Mariano Rubio. The Colonel, at the head of a regiment of Colombian hussars, turned the tide in this battle, waged entirely with sabers and lances, which paved the way for the no less famous action at Ayacucho, in which he also took part, receiving a wound. In 1827, it was his fate to fight boldly at Ituzaingó, under the immediate command of Alvear. In spite of his blood tie with the dictator Rosas, in later years he was one of Lavalle's men, and once broke up a troop of gaucho militia in an action the Colonel always referred to as a saberfest. With the defeat of the Unitarians, he emigrated to Uruguay, where he married. In the eighteen-forties, in the course of that country's long civil war, the Guerra Grande, he died in Montevideo during the siege of the city by Oribe's Blancos. He was nearly forty-four, which at that time was almost old age. He had been a friend of the writer Florencio Varela. It is quite likely that professors at the Military Academy would have flunked him, since his only experience lay in fighting battles, not in taking examinations. He left two daughters, of which the younger, María Justina, is the one who concerns us.

Toward the end of 1853, the Colonel's widow and his daughters settled in Buenos Aires. They never got back their lands, which had been confiscated by the dictator during the Colonel's long absence, but the memory of those miles and miles of lost acres on which they had never laid eyes survived in the family for many years. At the age of seventeen, María Justina married the physician Bernardo Jáuregui, who, though a civilian, fought during the civil wars in the battles of Pavón and Cepeda, and later died practicing his profession during the yellow-fever epidemic of the eighteen-seventies. He left a son and two daughters. Mariano, the firstborn, was a customs inspector, and he used to frequent the National Library and National Archives, with the intention of compiling an exhaustive life of the hero, his grandfather, which he never finished and perhaps never even began. The older daughter, María Elvira, married a cousin, a Saavedra, who was employed in the Ministry of Finance. Julia, the second daughter, had married a Mr. Molinari, who, despite his Italian name, was a professor of Latin and a person of the highest accomplishments. I pass over grandchildren and great-grandchildren; it is enough that my reader picture a family that is honorable, that has come down in life, and that is presided over by a heroic shade and by a daughter born in exile.

The family lived modestly in Palermo, in what at the time was the outskirts of Buenos Aires, not far from the church of Guadalupe. Mariano still remembered having seen there, from a tramcar of the Grand National Lines, the big pond on whose shores were scattered a series of hovels, not of galvanized-iron sheets but of unplastered brick. Yesterday's poverty was less poor than the poverty handed down to us today by industrialism. Fortunes were also much smaller then.

The Rubios lived above a local dry-goods store. The stairway was narrow; the bannister, which ran up the right-hand side, led to a longish corridor, at the end of which was a dark vestibule, where there were a coatrack and a few chairs. The vestibule opened into the small drawing room, with its upholstered furniture, and the drawing room into the dining room, with its mahogany furniture and glass-fronted china closet. The metal shutters, always kept drawn in fear of the sunlight, let a little dim twilight filter through. I recall an odor of stored-away things. At the back of the house were the bedrooms, the bathroom, a small gallery with a laundry tub, and the servant's room. In the whole house there were no books other than a volume of the poet Andrade; a short biography of the hero, with handwritten additions scribbled into the margins; and Montaner y Simón's *Hispano-American Encyclopedia*, acquired on installments, together with the small set of shelves that came with it. They lived on a pension, which was never paid them punctually, and on the income from a rented property—the single remains of the once vast acreage—in Lomas de Zamora.

At the time of my story, the elder lady lived with Julia, who was widowed, and with Julia's son. Mrs. Jáuregui went on hating bygone tyrants—Artigas, Rosas, and Urquiza. The First World War, which made her loathe the Germans, about whom she knew very little, was less real to her than the revolution of 1890 and, needless to say, the cavalry charge at Big Hill. Since 1932, she had been growing dimmer and dimmer; common metaphors are the best because they are the only true ones. She was, of course, a Catholic, which does not necessarily mean that she believed in a God that is One and is Three, or even in an afterlife. While her hands moved over her rosary, she muttered prayers that she had never understood. In place of Easter and of Twelfth Night she had accepted Christmas, just as she had grown to accept tea instead of maté. To her, the words "Protestant," "Jew," "Freemason," "heretic," and "atheist" were synonyms and empty of meaning. While she could still talk, she spoke not of Spaniards but of *godos*, or Goths, just as her ancestors had done. During the Centennial, in 1910, she could hardly believe that the Spanish Infanta—who, after all, was a princess—spoke, against all expectation, like a common Spaniard and not like an Argentine lady; it was at her son-in-law's wake that a rich relative, who had never set foot in the Jáuregui house but whose name they avidly sought in the society pages of the newspapers, gave her the disquieting news. Many of the place names that Mrs. Jáuregui used had long since been altered; she still spoke of such streets as Las Artes, Temple, Buen Orden, La Piedad, the two Calles Largas, and of the Plaza del Parque and the Portones. The family affected these archaisms, which in her were spontaneous. They spoke of "Orientales" instead of "Uruguayans."

Mrs. Jáuregui never went out of the house after 1921; perhaps she never suspected that Buenos Aires had been changing and growing. First memories are the most vivid. The city that she pictured beyond her front door may well have been a much earlier one than that of the time they were forced to move from the center of town out to Palermo. If so, to her the oxen that hauled wagons still rested in the square of the Once, and dead violets still spread their fragrance among the gardens of Barracas. "Now all my dreams are of dead people" was one of the last things she was heard to say. No one had ever thought of her as a fool, but as far as I know she had never enjoyed the pleasures of the mind; the last pleasures left her would be those of memory and, later on, of forgetfulness. She had always been generous. I recall her bright, quiet eyes and her smile. Who knows what tumult of passions—now lost but which once burned—there had been in that old woman; in her day, she had been quite pleasant-looking. Sensitive to plants, whose modest and silent life was so akin to her own, she looked after some begonias in her room and touched their leaves, which she could no longer see. Up until 1929, the year in which she sank into a kind of half sleep, she recounted historical happenings, but always using the same words in the same order, as if they were the Lord's Prayer, so that I grew to suspect there were no longer any real images behind them. Even eating one thing or another was all the same to her. She was, in short, happy.

Sleeping, as we all know, is the most secret of our acts. We devote a third of our lives to it, and yet do not understand it. For some, it is no more than an eclipse of wakefulness; for others, a more complex state spanning at one and the same time past, present, and future; for still others, an uninterrupted series of dreams. To say that Mrs. Jáuregui spent ten years in a quiet chaos is perhaps mistaken; each moment of those ten years may well have been a pure present, without a before or after. There is no reason to marvel at such a present, which we count by days and nights and by the hundreds of leaves of many calendars and by anxieties and events; it is what we go through every morning before waking up and every night before falling asleep. Twice each day, we are all the elder lady.

The Jáuregui family lived, as we have already seen, in a somewhat false situation. They felt they belonged to the aristocracy, but the people spoken of in the society column knew nothing whatever about them; they were descendants of a founding father, but more often than not the schoolbooks overlooked him. While it is undeniable that a street bore his name, that street, known to very few people, was lost somewhere out behind the sprawling Westside cemetery.

The fourteenth of January was drawing near. On the tenth,, an officer in full-dress uniform delivered to the family a letter signed by the Minister of War himself, announcing his visit on the fourteenth. The Jáureguis showed the letter to the whole neighborhood and made a great deal of the engraved stationery and the signature. Then the newspapermen came. The family helped them with all available information; it was obvious that they had never heard of Colonel Rubio. People whom the family scarcely knew called by telephone so as to be invited.

They all worked very hard for the great day. They waxed the floors, they washed the windows, they undraped the chandeliers, they polished the mahogany, they shined all the silver in the china closet, they moved the furniture around, and they opened the lid of the drawing-room piano to show off the velvet cloth that covered the keys. People came and went. A neighbor lady very kindly lent a pot of geraniums. The only person unaware of all the fuss was Mrs. Jáuregui, who, wearing a fixed smile, seemed not to understand a thing. Helped by the servant girl, Julia got her mother primped up as though she were already dead. The first things visitors would see on entering would be the oil portrait of the hero and, a little below it and to the right, the sword of his many battles. Even in hard times, the Jáureguis had always refused to sell the sword, thinking they would one day donate it to the Historical Museum.

The party would begin at seven. They had set the hour for six-thirty, knowing all along that nobody likes to be the first to arrive. By ten minutes past seven, not a soul had yet appeared; the family argued somewhat nervously the advantages and disadvantages of not being punctual. Elvira, who took pride in arriving on the dot, flatly stated that it was an unpardonable discourtesy to keep others waiting. Julia, repeating what her husband had always said, was of the opinion that arriving late was a courtesy, because if everyone did so it would make things easier and that way no one would be hurrying anyone else. At seven-fifteen, the house was packed. The whole neighborhood could see and envy the automobile and chauffeur of Mrs. Figueroa, who almost never invited the Jáureguis to her house but whom they received effusively, so that nobody would guess they only saw each other once in a blue moon. The President sent his aide, an extremely polite gentleman, who said that it was a great honor for him to shake the hand of the daughter of the hero of Big Hill. The Minister, who had to leave early, read a very fine speech, in which more was said about General San Martín, however, than about Colonel Rubio. The elderly lady sat in her armchair, propped up with pillows, and from time to time nodded her head approvingly or dropped her fan. A group of distinguished ladies, the Daughters of the Republic, sang her the National Anthem, which she seemed not to hear. The photographers herded the gathering into artistic groupings and were lavish with their flashbulbs. The small glasses of sherry and port were not enough to go around. Someone uncorked a number of bottles of champagne. Mrs. Jáuregui did not utter a single word; perhaps she no longer knew who she was. From that night on, she never left her bed.

When all the strangers had gone, the family improvised a small cold supper. The delicate perfume of incense had long since been dispelled by the odor of tobacco smoke and coffee.

The morning and afternoon papers loyally lied, dwelling on the almost miraculous memory of the hero's daughter, who "is an eloquent storehouse of a century of Argentine history." Julia wanted to show her mother the clippings. In her twilit room, the elder lady lay motionless, her eyes closed. She had no fever; the doctor examined her and said that everything was as it should be. A few days later, she died. The press of so many people, the unusual clamor, the flashbulbs, the speech, the uniforms, and the repeated handshaking had hastened her end. Perhaps she believed that they were Rosas' henchmen, who had broken into the house.

I think back on the dead soldiers of Big Hill; I think of the nameless men of America and of Spain who met their deaths under the hooves of the horses; I think that the last victim of that throng of lances high on a Peruvian tableland was, more than a century later, a very old lady.

Guayaquil

Guayaquil

Now I shall not journey to the Estado Occidental; now I shall not set eyes on snow-capped Higuerota mirrored in the waters of the Golfo Plácido; now I shall not decipher Bolívar's manuscripts in that library, which doubtless has its own shape and its own lengthening shadows but which from here in Buenos Aires I picture in so many different ways.

Rereading the above paragraph preparatory to writing the next, its at once melancholy and pompous tone troubles me. Perhaps one cannot speak of that Caribbean republic without, even from afar, echoing the monumental style of its most famous historian, Captain Joseph Korzeniowski—but in my case there is another reason. My opening paragraph, I suspect, was prompted by the unconscious need to infuse a note of pathos into a slightly painful and rather trivial episode. I shall with all probity recount what happened, and this may enable me to understand it. Furthermore, to confess to a thing is to leave off being an actor in it and to become an onlooker—to become somebody who has seen it and tells it and is no longer the doer.

The actual event took place last Friday, in this same room in which I am writing, at this same—though now slightly cooler—evening hour. Aware of our tendency to forget unpleasant things, I want to set down a written record of my conversation with Dr. Edward Zimmerman, of the University of Córdoba, before oblivion blurs the details. The memory I retain of that meeting is still quite vivid.

For the better understanding of my story, I shall have to set forth briefly the curious facts surrounding certain letters of General Bolívar's found among the papers of Dr. José Avellanos, whose *History of Fifty Years of Misrule*—thought to be lost under circumstances that are only too well known —was ultimately unearthed and published by his grandson, Dr. Ricardo Avellanos. To judge from references I have collected from various sources, these letters are of no particular interest, except for one dated from Cartagena on August 13, 1822, in which the Liberator places upon record details of his celebrated meeting with the Argentine national hero General San Martín. It is needless to underscore the value of this document; in it, Bolívar reveals—if only in part—exactly what had taken place during the two generals' interview the month before at Guayaquil. Dr. Ricardo Avellanos, embattled opponent of the government, refused to turn the correspondence over to his own country's Academy of History, and, instead, offered it for initial publication to a number of Latin American republics. Thanks to the praiseworthy zeal of our ambassador, Dr. Melaza-Mouton, the Argentine government was the first to accept Dr. Avellanos' disinterested offer. It was agreed that a delegate should be sent to Sulaco, the capital of the Estado Occidental, to transcribe the letters so as to see them into print upon return here. The rector of our university, in which I hold the chair of Latin American History, most generously recommended to the Minister of Education that I be appointed to carry out this mission. I also obtained the more or less unanimous vote of the National Academy of History, of which I am a member. The date of my audience with the Minister had already been fixed when it was learned that the University of Córdoba—which, I would rather suppose, knew nothing about these decisions —had proposed the name of Dr. Zimmerman.

Reference here, as the reader may be well aware, is to a foreign-born historian expelled from his country by the Third Reich and now an Argentine citizen. Of the doubtless noteworthy body of his work, I have glanced only at a vindication of the Semitic republic of Carthage—which posterity judges through the eyes of Roman historians, its enemies —and a sort of polemical essay which holds that government should be neither visible nor emotional. This proposal drew the unanswerable refutation of Martin Heidegger, who, using newspaper headlines, proved that the modern chief of state, far from being anonymous, is rather the protagonist, the choragus, the dancing David, who acts out the drama of his people with all the pomp of stagecraft, and resorts unhesitatingly to the overstatement inherent in the art of oration. He also proved that Zimmerman came of Hebrew, not to say Jewish, stock. Publication of this essay by the venerated existentialist was the immediate cause of the banishment and nomadic activities of our guest.

Needless to say, Zimmerman had come to Buenos Aires to speak to the Minister, who personally suggested to me, through one of his secretaries, that I see Zimmerman and, so as to avoid the unpleasant spectacle of two universities in disagreement, inform him of exactly how things stood. I of course agreed. Upon return home, I was told that Dr. Zimmerman had telephoned to announce his visit for six o'clock that same afternoon. I live, as everyone knows, on Chile Street. It was the dot of six when the bell rang.

With republican simplicity, I myself opened the door and

led him to my private study. He paused along the way to look at the patio; the black and white tiles, the two magnolias, and the wellhead stirred him to eloquence. He was, I believe, somewhat ill at ease. There was nothing out of the ordinary about him. He must have been forty or so, and seemed to have a biggish head. His eyes were hidden by dark glasses, which he once or twice left on the table, then snatched up again. When we first shook hands, I remarked to myself with a certain satisfaction that I was the taller, and at once I was ashamed of myself, for this was not a matter of a physical or even a moral duel but was simply to be an explanation of where things stood. I am not very observant—if I am observant at all—but he brought to mind what a certain poet has called, with an ugliness that matches what it defines, an "immoderate sartorial inelegance." I can still see garments of electric blue, with too many buttons and pockets. Zimmerman's tie, I noticed, was one of those conjuror's knots held in place by two plastic clips. He carried a leather portfolio, which I presumed was full of documents. He wore a short military moustache, and when in the course of our talk he lit a cigar I felt that there were too many things on that face. *Trop meublé*, I said to myself.

The successiveness of language—since every word occupies a place on the page and a moment in the reader's mind —tends to exaggerate what we are saying; beyond the visual trivia that I have listed, the man gave the impression of having experienced an arduous life.

On display in my study are an oval portrait of my great-grandfather, who fought in the wars of Independence, and some cabinets containing swords, medals, and flags. I showed Zimmerman those old glorious things, explaining as I went along; his eyes passed over them quickly, like one who is carrying out a duty, and, not without a hint of impoliteness that I believe was involuntary and mechanical, he interrupted and finished my sentences for me. He said, for example:

"Correct. Battle of Junín. August 6, 1824. Cavalry charge under Juárez."

"Under Suárez," I corrected.

I suspect his error was deliberate. He spread his arms in an Oriental gesture and exclaimed, "My first mistake, and certainly not my last! I feed on texts and slip up on facts—in you the interesting past lives." He pronounced his *v*'s like *f*'s.

Such flatteries displeased me. He was far more interested in my books, and let his eyes wander almost lovingly over the titles. I recall his saying, "Ah, Schopenhauer, who always disbelieved in history. This same set, edited by Grisebach, was the one I had in Prague. I thought I'd grow old in the friendship of those portable volumes, but it was history itself, in the flesh of a madman, that evicted me from that house and that city. Now here I am, with you, in South America, in this hospitable house of yours."

He spoke inelegantly but fluently, his noticeable German accent going hand in hand with a Spanish lisp. By then we were seated, and I seized upon what he had said in order to take up our subject. "History here in the Argentine is more merciful," I said. "I was born in this house and I expect to die here. Here my great-grandfather lay down his sword, which saw action throughout the continent. Here I have pondered the past and have compiled my books. I can almost say I've never been outside this library, but now I shall go abroad at last and travel to lands I have only traveled in maps." I cut short with a smile my possible rhetorical excess.

"Are you referring to a certain Caribbean republic?" said Zimmerman.

"So I am," I answered. "And it's to this imminent trip that I owe the honor of your visit."

Trinidad served us coffee. I went on slowly and confidently. "You probably know by now that the Minister has entrusted me with the mission of transcribing and writing an introduction to the new Bolívar letters, which have accidentally turned up in Dr. Avellanos' files. This mission, by a happy stroke, crowns my lifework—the work that somehow runs in my blood."

It was a relief having said what I had to say. Zimmerman appeared not to have heard me; his averted eyes were fixed not on my face but on the books at my back. He vaguely assented, and then spoke out, saying, "In your blood. You are the true historian. Your people roamed the length and breadth of this continent and fought in the great battles, while in obscurity mine were barely emerging from the ghetto. You, according to your own eloquent words, carry history in your blood; you have only to listen closely to an inner voice. I, on the other hand, must go all the way to Sulaco and struggle through stacks of perhaps apocryphal papers. Believe me, sir, I envy you."

His tone was neither challenging nor mocking; his words were the expression of a will that made of the future something as irrevocable as the past. His arguments hardly mattered. The strength lay in the man himself, not in them. Zimmerman continued, with a schoolteacher's deliberation: "In this matter of Bolívar—I beg your pardon, San Martín—your stand, *cher maître*, is known to all scholars. *Votre siège est fait.* As yet, I have not examined Bolívar's pertinent letter, but it is obvious, or reasonable to guess, that it was written as a piece of self-justification. In any case, this much-touted letter will show us only Bolívar's side of the question, not San Martín's. Once made public, it should be weighed in the balance, studied, passed through the sieve of criticism, and, if need be, refuted. No one is better qualified for that final judgment than you, with your magnifying glass. The scalpel, the lancet—scientific rigor itself demands them! Allow me at the same time to point out that the name of the editor of the letter will remain linked to the letter. Such a link is hardly going to stand you in good stead. The public at large will never bother to look into these subtleties."

I realize now that what we argued after that, in the main, was useless. Maybe I felt it at the time. In order to avoid an outright confrontation I grasped at a detail, and I asked him whether he really thought the letters were fakes.

"That they are in Bolívar's own hand," he said, "does not necessarily mean that the whole truth is to be found in them. For all we know, Bolívar may have tried to deceive the recipient of the letter or, simply, may have deceived himself. You, a historian, a thinker, know far better than I that the mystery lies in ourselves, not in our words."

These pompous generalities irritated me, and I dryly remarked that within the riddle that surrounded us, the meeting at Guayaquil—in which General San Martín renounced mere ambition and left the destiny of South America in the hands of Bolívar—was also a riddle possibly not unworthy of our attention.

"The interpretations are so many," Zimmerman said. "Some historians believe San Martín fell into a trap; others, like Sarmiento, have it that he was a European soldier at loose ends on a continent he never understood; others again—for the most part Argentines—ascribe to him an act of self-denial; still others, weariness. We also hear of the secret order of who knows what Masonic lodge."

I said that, at any rate, it would be interesting to have the exact words spoken between San Martín, the Protector of Peru, and Bolívar, the Liberator. Zimmerman delivered his judgment.

"Perhaps the words they exchanged were irrelevant," he said. "Two men met face to face at Guayaquil; if one of them was master, it was because of his stronger will, not because of the weight of arguments. As you see, I have not forgotten my Schopenhauer." He added, with a smile, "Words, words, words. Shakespeare, insuperable master of words, held them in scorn. In Guayaquil or in Buenos Aires—in Prague, for that matter—words always count less than persons."

At that moment I felt that something was happening between us, or, rather, that something had already happened. In some uncanny way we were already two other people. The dusk entered into the room, and I had not lit the lamps. By chance, I asked, "You are from Prague, Doctor?"

"I *was* from Prague," he answered.

To skirt the real subject, I said, "It must be an unusual city. I've never been there, but the first book I ever read in German was Meyrink's novel *Der Golem*."

"It's the only book by Gustav Meyrink worth remembering," Zimmerman said. "It's wiser not to attempt the others, compounded as they are of bad writing and worse theosophy. All in all, something of the strangeness of Prague stalks the pages of that book of dreams within dreams. Everything is strange in Prague, or, if you prefer, nothing is strange. Anything may happen there. In London, on certain evenings, I have had the same feeling."

"You have spoken of the will," I said. "In the tales of the Mabinogion, two kings play chess on the summit of a hill, while below them their warriors fight. One of the kings wins the game; a rider comes to him with the news that the army of the other side has been beaten. The battle of the men was a mirror of the battle of the chessboard."

"Ah, a feat of magic," said Zimmerman.

"Or the display of a will in two different fields," I said. "Another Celtic legend tells of the duel between two famous bards. One, accompanying himself on the harp, sings from the twilight of morning to the twilight of evening. Then, under the stars or moon, he hands his harp over to his rival. The second bard lays the instrument aside and gets to his feet. The first bard acknowledges defeat."

"What erudition, what power of synthesis!" exclaimed Zimmerman. Then he added, more calmly, "I must confess my ignorance, my lamentable ignorance, of Celtic lore. You, like the day, span East and West, while I am held to my little Carthaginian corner, complemented now with a smattering of Latin American history. I am a mere plodder."

In his voice were both Jewish and German servility, but I felt, insofar as victory was already his, that it cost him very little to flatter me or to admit I was right. He begged me not to trouble myself over the arrangements for his trip. ("Provisions" was the actual word he used.) On the spot, he drew out of his portfolio a letter addressed to the Minister. In it, I expounded the motives behind my resignation, and I acknowledged Dr. Zimmerman's indisputable merits. Zimmerman put his own fountain pen in my hand for my signature. When he put the letter away, I could not help catching a glimpse of his passage aboard the next day's Buenos Aires–Sulaco flight.

On his way out he paused again before the volumes of Schopenhauer, saying, "Our master, our common master, denied the existence of involuntary acts. If you stay behind in this house—in this spacious, patrician home—it is because down deep inside you want to remain here. I obey, and I thank you for your will."

Taking this last pittance without a word, I accompanied him to the front door. There, as we said goodbye, he remarked, "The coffee was excellent."

I go over these hasty jottings, which will soon be consigned to the flames. Our meeting had been short. I have the feeling that I shall give up any future writing. *Mon siège est fait.*

Doctor Brodie's Report

Doctor Brodie's Report

Among the pages of one of the volumes of Lane's *Arabian Nights' Entertainments* (London, 1839), a set of which my dear friend Paul Keins turned up for me, we made the discovery of the manuscript I am about to transcribe below. The neat handwriting—an art which typewriters are now helping us to forget—suggests that it was composed some time around that same date. Lane's work, as is well known, is lavish with extensive explanatory notes; in the margins of my copy there are a number of annotations, interrogation marks, and now and then emendations written in the same hand as the manuscript. We may surmise that the wondrous tales of Shahrazad interested the annotator less than the customs of the Mohammedans. Of David Brodie, D.D., whose signature adorns the bottom of the last page with a fine flourish, I have been unable to uncover any information except that he was a Scottish missionary, born in Aberdeen, who preached the Christian faith first in the heart of Africa and later on in certain backlying regions of Brazil, a land he was probably led to by his knowledge of Portuguese. I am unaware of the place and date of his death. The manuscript, as far as I know, was never given to the press.

What follows is a faithful transcription of his report, composed in a rather colorless English, with no other omissions than two or three Bible verses jotted in the margins and a curious passage concerning the sexual practices of the Yahoos, which our good Presbyterian discreetly committed to Latin. The first page is missing.

———

. . . of the region infested by Ape-men dwell the "Mlch," * whom I shall call Yahoos so that my readers will be reminded of their bestial nature and also because, given the total absence of vowels in their harsh language, an exact transliteration is virtually impossible. Including the "Nr," who dwell farther to the south in the thorn-bush, the numbers of the tribe do not, I believe, exceed seven hundred. The cipher which I propose is a mere conjecture, since, save for the king and queen and the witch doctors, the Yahoos sleep in no fixed abode but wherever night overtakes them. Swamp fever and the continual incursions of the Ape-men diminish their number. Only a very few individuals have names. In order to address one another, it is their custom to fling a small handful of mud. I have also noticed Yahoos who, to attract a friend's attention, throw themselves on the ground and wallow in the dust. Save for their lower foreheads and for having a peculiar copperish hue that reduces their blackness, in other physical respects they do not noticeably differ from the "Kroo." They take their nourishment from fruits, root-stalks, and the smaller reptiles; they imbibe the milk of cats and of chiropterans; and they fish with their hands. While eating, they normally conceal themselves or else close their eyes. All other physical habits they perform in open view, much the same as

* I give the "ch" the value it has in the word "loch." [Author's note.]

the Cynics of old. . . . So as to partake of their wisdom, they devour the raw corpses of their witch doctors and of the royal family. When I admonished them for this evil custom they touched their lips and their bellies, perhaps to indicate that the dead are also edible, or—but this explanation may be farfetched—in order that I might come to understand that everything we eat becomes, in the long run, human flesh. In their warfare they employ stones, which they gather for that purpose, and magical spells and incantations. They go about quite naked, the arts of clothing and tattooing being altogether unknown to them.

It is worthy of note that, though they have at hand a wide, grassy plateau on which there are springs of clear water and shade-dispensing trees, they prefer to swarm in the marshlands which surround this eminence, as if delighting in the rigors of the hot climate and the general unwholesomeness. The slopes of the plateau are steep and could easily be utilized as a natural bulwark against the onslaughts of the Apemen. The clans of Scotland, in similar circumstances, erected their castles on the summits of hills; I advised the witch doctors to adopt this simple defensive measure, but my words were of no avail. They allowed me, however, to build a hut for myself on higher ground, where the night air is cooler.

The tribe is ruled over by a king, whose power is absolute, but it is my suspicion that the true rulers are the witch doctors, who administer to him and who have chosen him. Every male born into the tribe is subjected to a painstaking examination; if he exhibits certain stigmata, the nature of which were not revealed to me, he is elevated to the rank of king of the Yahoos. So that the physical world may not lead him from the paths of wisdom, he is gelded on the spot, his eyes are burned, and his hands and feet are amputated. Thereafter, he lives confined in a cavern called the Castle ("Qzr"), into which only the four witch doctors and the two slave women who attend him and anoint him with dung are permitted entrance. Should war arise, the witch doctors remove him from his cavern, display him to the tribe to excite their courage, and bear him, lifted onto their shoulders after the manner of a flag or a talisman, to the thick of the fight. In such cases, he dies almost immediately under the hail of stones flung at him by the Ape-men.

In another Castle lives the queen, who is not permitted to see her king. During my sojourn, this lady was kind enough to receive me; she was smiling, young, and, insofar as her race allowed, graceful. Bracelets of metalwork and of ivory and necklaces of teeth adorned her nakedness. She inspected me, sniffed me, and, after touching me with a finger, ended by offering herself to me in the presence of all her retinue. My cloth and my ethics, however, forbade me that honor, which commonly she grants only to the witch doctors and to the slave hunters, for the most part Muslims, whose caravans journey across the kingdom. Twice or thrice she sank a gold pin into my flesh; such prickings being tokens of royal favor, the number of Yahoos are more than a few who stick themselves with pins to encourage the belief that the queen herself pricked them. The ornaments she wore, and which I have described, come from other regions. Since they lack the capacity to fashion the simplest object, the Yahoos regard such ornaments as natural. To the tribe my hut was a tree, despite the fact that many of them saw me construct it and even lent me their aid. Amongst a number of other items, I had in my possession a watch, a cork helmet, a mariner's compass, and a Bible. The Yahoos stared at them, weighed them in their hands, and wanted to know where I had found them. They customarily reached for my cutlass not by the hilt but by the blade, seeing it, undoubtedly, in their own way, which causes me to wonder to what degree they would be able to perceive a chair. A house of several rooms would strike them as a maze, though perhaps they might find their way inside it in the manner of the cat, though the cat does not imagine the house. My beard, which then was red, was a source of wonderment to them all, and it was with obvious fondness that they stroked it.

The Yahoos are insensitive to pain and pleasure, save for the relishment they get from raw and rancid meat and evil-smelling things. An utter lack of imagination moves them to cruelty.

I have spoken of the queen and the king; I shall speak now of the witch doctors. I have already recorded that they are four, this number being the largest that their arithmetic spans. On their fingers they count thus: one, two, three, four, *many*. Infinity begins at the thumb. The same, I am informed, occurs among the Indian tribes who roam in the vicinity of Buenos-Ayres on the South American continent. In spite of the fact that four is the highest number at their disposal, the Arabs who trade with them do not swindle them, because in the bartering everything is divided into lots—which each of the traders piles by his side—of one, two, three, and four. Such transactions are cumbersome, but they do not admit of error or fraudulence. Of the entire nation of the Yahoos, the witch doctors are the only persons who have aroused my interest. The tribesmen attribute to them the power of transforming into ants or into turtles anyone who so desires; one individual, who detected my disbelief, pointed out an ant-hill to me, as though that constituted a proof.

Memory is greatly defective among the Yahoos, or perhaps is altogether nonexistent. They speak of the havoc wrought by an invasion of leopards, but do not know who witnessed the event, they or their fathers, nor do they know whether they are recounting a dream. The witch doctors show some signs of memory, albeit to a reduced degree; they are able to recollect in the evening things which took place that morning or the preceding evening. They are also endowed with the faculty of foresight, and can state with quiet confidence what will happen ten or fifteen minutes hence. They convey, for example, that "A fly will graze the nape of my neck" or "In a moment we shall hear the song of a bird." Hundreds of times I have borne witness to this curious gift, and I have also reflected upon it at length. Knowing that past, present, and future already exist, detail upon detail, in God's prophetic memory, in His Eternity, what baffles me is that men, while they can look indefinitely backward, are not allowed to look one whit forward. If I am able to remember in all vividness that towering four-master from Norway which I saw when I was scarcely four, why am I taken aback by the fact that man may be capable of foreseeing what is about to happen? To the philosophical mind, memory is as much a wonder as divination; tomorrow morning is closer to us than the crossing of the Red Sea by the Hebrews, which, nevertheless, we remember.

The tribesmen are proscribed from lifting their gaze to the stars, a privilege accorded only to the witch doctors. Each witch doctor has a disciple, whom he instructs from childhood in secret lore and who succeeds him upon his death. In this wise they are always four, a number of magical properties, since it is the highest to which the Yahoo mind attains. They profess, in their own fashion, the doctrines of heaven and hell. Both places are subterranean. Hell, which is dry and filled with light, harbours the sick, the aged, the ill-treated, the Ape-men, the Arabs, and the leopards; heaven, which is depicted as marshy and beclouded, is the dwelling-place of the king and queen, the witch doctors, and those who have been happy, merciless, and blood-thirsty on earth. They worship as well a god whose name is "Dung," and whom possibly they have conceived in the image and semblance of the king; he is a blind, mutilated, stunted being, and enjoys limitless powers. Dung is wont to take the form of an ant or a serpent.

After the foregoing remarks, it should cause no one to wonder that during my long stay among them I did not contrive to convert a single Yahoo. The words "Our father," owing to the fact that they have no notion of fatherhood, left them puzzled. They cannot, it seems, accept a cause so remote and so unlikely, and are therefore uncomprehending that an act carried out several months before may bear relation to the birth of a child. Moreover, all the women engage in carnal commerce, and not all are mothers.

The Yahoo language is complex, having affinities with no others of which I have any knowledge. We cannot speak even of parts of speech, for there are no parts. Each monosyllabic word corresponds to a general idea whose specific meaning depends on the context or upon accompanying grimaces. The word "nrz," for example, suggests dispersion or spots, and may stand for the starry sky, a leopard, a flock of birds, smallpox, something bespattered, the act of scattering, or the flight that follows defeat in warfare. "Hrl," on the other hand, means something compact or dense. It may stand for the tribe, a tree trunk, a stone, a heap of stones, the act of heaping stones, the gathering of the four witch doctors, carnal conjunction, or a forest. Pronounced in another manner or accompanied by other grimaces, each word may hold an opposite meaning. Let us not be unduly amazed; in our own tongue, the verb "to cleave" means both to divide asunder and to adhere. Of course, among the Yahoos, there are no sentences, nor even short phrases.

The intellectual power to draw abstractions which such a language assumes has led me to believe that the Yahoos, for all their backwardness, are not a primitive but a degenerate nation. This conjecture is borne out by the inscriptions I discovered on the heights of the plateau and whose characters, which are not unlike the runes carved by our forefathers, are no longer within the tribe's capacity to decipher. It is as though the tribe had forgotten written language and found itself reduced now only to the spoken word.

The diversions of these people are the fights which they stage between trained cats, and capital executions. Someone is accused of an attempt against the queen's chastity, or of having eaten in the sight of another; without either the testimony of witnesses or a confession, the king finds a verdict of guilty. The condemned man suffers tortures that I shall do my best to forget, and then is stoned to death. The queen is privileged to cast the first stone and, what is usually superfluous, the last. The throng applauds her skill and the beauty of her parts, and, all in a frenzy, acclaims her, pelting her with roses and fetid things. The queen, without uttering a sound, smiles.

Another of the tribe's customs is the discovery of poets. Six or seven words, generally enigmatic, may come to a man's mind. He cannot contain himself and shouts them out, standing in the center of a circle formed by the witch doctors and the common people, who are stretched out on the ground. If the poem does not stir them, nothing comes to pass, but if the poet's words strike them they all draw away from him, without a sound, under the command of a holy dread. Feeling then that the spirit has touched him, nobody, not even his own mother, will either speak to him or cast a glance at him. Now he is a man no longer but a god, and anyone has license to kill him. The poet, if he has his wits about him, seeks refuge in the sand-dunes of the North.

I have already described how I came to the land of the Yahoos. It will be recalled that they encircled me, that I discharged my firearm into the air, and that they took the discharge for a kind of magical thunderclap. In order to foster that error, I strove thereafter to go about without my weapon. One spring morning, at the break of day, we were suddenly overrun by the Ape-men; I started down from the highlands, gun in hand, and killed two of these animals. The rest fled in amazement. Shot, it is known, is invisible. For the first time in my life I heard myself cheered. It was then, I believe, that the queen received me. The memory of the Yahoos, as I have mentioned, being undependable, that very afternoon I made good an escape. My subsequent adventures in the jungle are of little account. In due course, I came upon a village of black men who knew how to plough, to sow, and to pray, and with whom I made myself understood in Portuguese. A Romish missionary, Father Fernandes, offered me the hospitality of his hut, and cared for me until I was able to continue on my hard journey. At first I found it revolting to see him open his mouth without the slightest dissimulation and put into it pieces of food. I still covered my mouth with my hand, or averted my eyes; a few days later, however, I had readjusted myself. I recall with distinct pleasure our debates in topics theological, but I had no success in turning him to the true faith of Jesus.

I set down this account now in Glasgow. I have told of my visit among the Yahoos, but have not dwelt upon the essential horror of the experience, which never ceases entirely to be with me, and which visits me yet in dreams. In the street, upon occasion, I feel that they still surround me. Only too well do I know the Yahoos to be a barbarous nation, perhaps the most barbarous to be found upon the face of the earth, but it would be unjust to overlook certain traits which redeem them. They have institutions of their own; they enjoy a king; they employ a language based upon abstract concepts; they believe, like the Hebrews and the Greeks, in the divine nature of poetry; and they surmise that the soul survives the death of the body. They also uphold the truth of punishments and rewards. After their fashion, they stand for civilization much as we ourselves do, in spite of our many transgressions. I do not repent having fought in their ranks against the Ape-men. Not only is it our duty to save their souls, but it is my fervent prayer that the Government of Her Majesty will not ignore what this report makes bold to suggest.

Afterword

Afterword

It is a known fact that the word "invention" originally stood for "discovery," and thus the Roman Church celebrates the Invention of the Cross, not its unearthing, or discovery. Behind this etymological shift we may, I think, glimpse the whole Platonic doctrine of archetypes—of all things being already there. William Morris thought that the essential stories of man's imagination had long since been told and that by now the storyteller's craft lay in rethinking and retelling them. His *Earthly Paradise* is a token of the theory, though not, of course, a proof. I do not go as far as Morris went, but to me the writing of a story has more of discovery about it than of deliberate invention.

Walking down the street or along the galleries of the National Library, I feel that something is about to take over in me. That something may be a tale or a poem. I do not tamper with it; I let it have its way. From afar, I sense it taking shape. I dimly see its end and beginning but not the dark gap in between. This middle, in my case, is given me gradually. If its discovery happens to be withheld by the gods, my conscious self has to intrude, and these unavoidable makeshifts are, I suspect, my weakest pages.

"The Intruder," the first written of these new stories of mine, haunted me for some thirty years before I set it down. At first, all I had was the idea of two brothers and a woman, loved by them both, who in the end had to be sacrificed to their friendship. Initially, I wanted a California setting, but as I knew—and so would my readers—that my knowledge of California was merely bookish, the credibility of the tale would have been impaired. I finally kept to Buenos Aires.

In my Preface, I mention a hidden link between two of the stories. Now I can say openly that I meant "Juan Muraña" and "The Meeting." Underlying both of them is the fancy that a weapon, in time, may have a secret life of its own. In "Juan Muraña," we also get the idea of a man, after death, becoming a thing—of a knife fighter being his knife.

Three of the stories are taken from life. The elder lady who presides over one of these was—may I confide this to the reader?—a great-aunt of mine. In another, a certain duel is still being fought with a fine grace by the two antagonists. The tale of the two gauchos whose throats were cut and who were then made to run a race actually took place a century ago in Uruguay.

"The Unworthy Friend" is really a confession. During my schooldays in Geneva, a companion whom I looked on as a hero offered me his friendship. I thrust it aside thinking his offer was a mistake, since I did not deserve it. Out of that personal experience came the tale of the Jewish boy in a Buenos Aires slum.

"Rosendo's Tale" is, I think, a fair rendering of what actually happened, or might have happened, in an early and all-too-famous extravaganza of mine called "Streetcorner Man." In the new version I have done my best to hark back to sanity.

"Guayaquil" can be read in two different ways—as a symbol of the meeting of the famous generals, or, if the reader is in a magical mood, as the transformation of the two historians into the two dead generals.

In most cases, my stories are woven around a plot. In "The Elder Lady" and in "The Duel" I have attempted something else. I have tried, after the manner of Henry James, to build these tales around a situation or a character.

Since 1953, after a longish interval of composing only poems and short prose pieces, these are the first stories I have written.

J. L. B.

Buenos Aires, December 29, 1970

Bibliographical Note

The original titles and first magazine or newspaper appearances of the stories in this volume as follows (place of publication, throughout, is Buenos Aires):

THE MEETING: "El encuentro," *La Prensa* (October 5, 1969).

ROSENDO'S TALE: "Historia de Rosendo Juárez," *La Nación* (November 9, 1969).

JUAN MURAÑA: "Juan Muraña," *La Prensa* (March 29, 1970).

THE END OF THE DUEL: "El otro duelo," *Los Libros* (August 1970).

THE GOSPEL ACCORDING TO MARK: "El evangelio según Marcos," *La Nación* (August 2, 1970).

GUAYAQUIL: "Guayaquil," *Periscopio* (August 4, 1970).

"El indigno" (THE UNWORTHY FRIEND), "La señora mayor" (THE ELDER LADY), and "El informe de Brodie" (DOCTOR BRODIE'S REPORT) did not appear anywhere before their publication in book form. "La intrusa" (THE INTRUDER) was first published in an edition of fifty-two copies illustrated by Emilio Centurión and privately printed by the Buenos Aires bibliophile Gustavo Fillol Day in April 1966. It also appeared, the same month, in the sixth impression of the third edition of *El Aleph* (Emecé, 1966), where it continued to appear until the twelfth impression, issued November 1970; here it was removed from the text but is erroneously listed in the table of contents. "El duelo" (THE DUEL) made its first appearance, with an illustration by Santiago Cogorno, in an edition of twenty-five copies; it was printed by Juan

Osvaldo Viviano, another Buenos Aires bibliophile, in April 1970, for private distribution among his friends.

With the exception of "La intrusa," these stories were collected for the first time in *El informe de Brodie*. "La intrusa" was slightly revised for its inclusion in the *Brodie* volume, as were certain other pieces in the book's third and fourth printings.

El informe de Brodie was published by Emecé Editores on August 7, 1970.